the romantic comedies

Puppy Love

NANCY KRULIK

Simon Pulse

New York London Toronto Sydney

This book is a work of fiction. Any references to historical events, real people, or real locales are used fictitiously. Other names, characters, places, and incidents are the product of the author's imagination, and any resemblance to actual events or locales or persons, living or dead, is entirely coincidental.

SIMON PULSE
An imprint of Simon & Schuster Children's Publishing Division
1230 Avenue of the Americas, New York, NY 10020
Copyright © 2008 by Nancy Krulik
All rights reserved, including the right of reproduction in whole or in part in any form.
SIMON PULSE and colophon are registered trademarks of Simon & Schuster, Inc.
Designed by Ann Zeak
The text of this book was set in Garamond 3.
Manufactured in the United States of America
First Simon Pulse edition August 2008
10 9 8 7 6 5 4 3 2 1
Library of Congress Control Number 2008922277
ISBN-13: 978-1-4424-3079-2

For Pepper, who walks me every day

One

"Come on, you guys, *sit*. We have to wait until Curly pees." Alana Marks used a stern but calm voice to control three of her four charges, Nicolette, Frisky, and Noodles, as they waited for Curly to do her business near a bench in Central Park. "You've all had your turn. Now it's hers."

The bird-watchers standing nearby shot her an evil look. Alana sighed. She had a feeling they weren't too happy with her. The bird people never were. Not that she blamed them. After all, there was no chance any of the yellow-bellied sapsuckers or white-throated sparrows they were seeking would come near as long as there were four dogs around—especially four dogs who were as rambunctious as Nicolette, Frisky, Noodles, and Curly. Alana had been standing there only a few seconds, and already Nicolette (the poodle) was growling angrily under her breath, Frisky (the Jack Russell terrier) was bouncing up and down like a jumping bean, and Noodles (the bulldog) was eyeing a mud puddle with far too much interest for Alana's taste.

She just didn't get it. Other dog walkers always seemed so in charge of their clients. But it seemed like her dogs were always out of control. Then again, maybe it wasn't that the *dogs* were out of control. Maybe it was just that *they* were controlling *her*. Either way, it was not a great position for a dog walker to be in.

Alana held tight to the four leashes and watched as Curly scratched at the gray dirt with her back paws and then looked up at her, ready to walk. Alana smiled. "Good girl," she complimented the golden-haired cocker spaniel. Curly raised her head proudly and glanced in the direction of the other dogs, as though she were making sure they'd heard her being praised. Alana giggled. Curly could be such a diva.

Alana had spent seventeen years—her

whole life—in Manhattan, growing up not far from the park, at Ninety-fifth and Columbus, but the Ramble section of Central Park never ceased to amaze her. The moment she stepped off the main road and into the wooded area, she felt as though she were in the woods. In fact, she often remarked that it "smelled like camp" in the Ramble, particularly right after it rained. It *felt* like a summer camp too—the thick trees, winding dirt paths, and babbling brooks were all like something you'd find in the Poconos or somewhere. In fact, if you didn't look up, you'd never know you were in New York City anymore. But the minute you did, there was no mistaking the huge skyscrapers that surrounded all of Central Park, towering over the haven like a giant concrete and glass fortress.

"Arooooo."

"Grrr!"

Alana was suddenly shaken from her thoughts by some wild jumping on the other end of the leashes. She looked in the dogs' direction and discovered the impetus for the sudden canine rebellion. A squirrel. A tiny, little gray squirrel. Too small to do any damage to anyone. At least that's what you'd think if you weren't a dog walker. But Alana knew better. "Uh-oh," she murmured, fully aware of the effect squirrels had on the dogs.

For a moment all four dogs just stood there, watching. The squirrel stared back, afraid to move. Then, suddenly, it gathered the courage to make a run for it and scampered quickly in the direction of a nearby tree. . . .

Frisky was the first of the dogs to take action. He began bouncing up and down wildly, tugging on his leash in an attempt to run after the squirrel. Not to be outdone, Curly barked wildly and pulled at her leash, trying to get Alana to follow behind as she raced toward the thick tree at the end of the hill, to where the frightened gray squirrel had darted.

Nicolette, however, had spotted a second squirrel off to the right, and she was determined to get *that* one. Noodles didn't care which of the two squirrels he captured, as long as he got to chase something. As far as the bulldog was concerned, the majority ruled.

"WHOAAA!" Alana's voice echoed through the Ramble as the dogs took off in search of their prey. She could feel the leashes slipping from her grip as the dogs pulled her behind them, but she refused to let go. She was going to hold on to those dogs no matter what. Even if "no matter what" meant losing her footing and sliding headfirst on her stomach down a huge hill. "STOP!" Alana shouted as she slid downhill. "HEEL! NO! PLAY DEAD!" Any command, just to get them to stop.

And they did stop—with such a sudden force that Alana just missed slamming her head into a nearby tree. Still, she was pretty proud of herself. She'd finally gotten the dogs to obey her.

Or not. On closer inspection she discovered that the dogs had stopped only because they'd spotted a hot dog on the ground. At the moment, they were sharing the frankfurter and its accompanying bun with great glee. Alana knew that Mrs. Stanhope, Nicolette's owner, would be especially upset about the hot dog. Nicolette ate only gourmet dog food, bought at top price from the Barkery, an elite dog shop on Broadway. Actually, Nicolette did sometimes get people food—but even then the prized poodle was fed only the finest cuts of steak. Still, at the moment, Alana didn't care if Nicolette ate something as pedestrian as a dirty frankfurter. The poodle seemed happy enough. And at least she was standing still. They all were.

But that wouldn't last long, and Alana knew it. Quickly the slender teen leaped to her feet and brushed her long, golden brown hair from her face. Looking down at her grass-stained white T-shirt and dark blue tight "skinny" jeans, she groaned. Darn it! Brand-new jeans, and now they had a huge hole in the knee. She'd probably torn them on a rock as she went down the hill—which would also explain the small trickle of blood coming from the cut on her knee. "Thanks so much, you guys," she grumbled sarcastically. But she couldn't stay angry with them for long. She never could. Alana had a real soft spot when it came to dogs. She adored them for their loyalty, their love, and their uncanny ability to know exactly when she needed a little canine comfort.

In fact, at just that moment, Curly, possibly sensing Alana's dismay, padded over to her and rubbed her soft furry body against Alana's calves. Then she looked up and gave her a smile. A genuine smile; the kind only a dog can pull off. And of course it melted Alana's heart. "I'm okay, Curly," she said gently as she pulled a leaf from her bangs.

Alana glanced around quickly. No one seemed to be around. That was something anyway. Nobody had actually seen her free-fall down the grassy hill. She wasn't going to wind up in some amateur videographer's joke video on YouTube or anything. Thank goodness for small favors.

"Time to go home," Alana told the dogs as she began walking toward the exit of the park. For once, Nicolette, Curly, Noodles, and Frisky did as they were told, walking in unison toward Central Park West. It was as though their acute canine senses told them that they had gone too far this time and they'd better mind their manners. Alana was able to stroll toward the West Seventy-seventh Street exit of the park without incident.

As she reached the corner of Seventy-seventh and Central Park West, a big red double-decker tour bus pulled up. As it stopped at the red light, Alana could hear the tour guide's voice ringing out from the microphone. "And to your left is the American Museum of Natural History."

Almost immediately the tourists on the top deck pulled out their cameras and began clicking away.

The odd thing was, the tourists were aiming their lenses to the right of the bus, not the left. They weren't shooting the huge stone museum; they were taking shots of Alana. For some reason they seemed to think that a grass-stained dog walker with ripped jeans, a bloody knee, and leaves in her hair was more interesting than the big statue of Teddy Roosevelt outside the museum. *Haven't these people ever seen a dog walker before?*

Apparently not, from the sound of the clicking cameras. Suddenly she'd become a tourist attraction! She could just see the guidebooks now—"Things you can't miss on your trip to New York: the Statue of Liberty, Ellis Island, the Empire State Building, and Alana Marks being pulled down the street by four wild and crazy dogs."

"Come on, you guys, let's move a little faster," Alana said as she urged the pups to walk up the block toward West Eighty-first Street. She waved at the tour bus as she and the dogs strolled by. "May as well give them a real show."

A few hours later Alana found herself sitting in her best friend, Stella's, bedroom, with her high school physics book in hand. "As if this day wasn't lousy enough, we've got all this science homework to do by tomorrow," she groaned. "And I don't understand any of it."

"Hang in there," Stella replied. "Just a few more months and we'll be accepted into college. Then we can develop major cases of senioritis."

Alana sighed. "We're seniors. Can you believe it?"

"It's been two weeks already. I think the idea's kind of sunk in," Stella replied.

"It's just not what I thought it would be," Alana explained to her. "I don't feel like a senior. Now, last year's seniors—they were really the kings and queens of the school. But we're just . . . us." Alana frowned slightly as the thought of one of last year's seniors leaped immediately to mind. Sammy Arden had been Alana's boyfriend for three years—they'd met when he was a sophomore and she was just a lowly freshman. But now Sammy had graduated from Lincoln High and was attending Columbia University. Alana suspected his absence at

Lincoln was part of the reason things just didn't seem the way she thought they would during her senior year. Instead of feeling like the queen of the school, she still felt kind of young in comparison.

"Last year's seniors probably felt like they were just *them*, too," Stella suggested. "Nothing changed about them when they became seniors, except the way everyone else in the school thought of them. This year's juniors are probably looking up to us in the same way."

Alana nodded. "I guess," she said. She wiped a few beads of sweat from her forehead. It was the third week in September, but apparently nobody had told New York City that summer was over. The temperature had to be at least eighty today, and it felt even warmer in Stella's small back bedroom. "Can you turn on the air-conditioning?" she asked her friend.

Stella shook her head. "Do you have any idea how much energy that air conditioner uses?"

"But it's so hot out," Alana insisted.

"And do you know *why* it's so hot today?" Stella demanded.

Alana rolled her eyes. *Here it comes.*

"Because of global warming," Stella continued. "And we have global warming because people in this country can't stand a little bit of discomfort, even if it means saving the planet. Air conditioners run on electricity, and most electricity is powered by coal. That sends carbon into—"

Just then Alana's cell phone began to ring. *At the end of the world, you're the last thing I see. . . ."* Alana giggled slightly. Her My Chemical Romance ring tone was completely apropos for this particular conversation. She was thrilled to hear her phone go off in the middle of Stella's latest environmental tirade. Not that she didn't appreciate her best friend's passion for the planet, but after a while . . .

"It's Sammy," Alana announced happily, her heart pumping just a little faster as she checked the caller ID.

"Ah, the college man is calling," Stella teased.

Alana instinctively ran her fingers through her hair and glanced in the mirror above Stella's desk.

"Relax, it's the phone, he can't see you," Stella joked. "But he'll hang up if you don't answer soon."

Alana blushed, embarrassed to be caught primping for a phone call—even if it was only by her best friend. But she did take Stella's advice and answered the phone immediately. "Hey, there," she said, trying to sound sophisticated and calm as she answered his call, even though she felt anything but.

"Hi, hon, how's it goin'?"

Alana relaxed immediately at the sound of his voice. Talking to Sammy was like slipping into her favorite pair of jeans—it just always felt right. Which was to be expected. Sammy was, after all, her first love. *Probably the love of her life.* She was supposed to feel relaxed and comfortable with him.

"I've had better days," Alana admitted. "The dogs went a little nuts in the park . . ."

"Oh," Sammy interrupted her, sounding only partly interested. "Well, this should cheer you up. I got an A- on my first persuasive essay for Comp 101!"

"An A-, whoa!" Alana complimented him. "That totally rocks."

"I used that idea you gave me," Sammy told her. "You know, the one about the importance of educating the children of immigrants."

Alana smiled, pleased that she had played a part in Sammy's first collegiate success.

"Of course, I added a lot of information you didn't have. A college paper has to be a lot more intense than a high school essay," Sammy continued.

"I'm sure," Alana agreed. "And I'll bet it helped that the subject was something you really believed in. That always comes through when you're writing a paper."

"Mmm, I guess," Sammy replied non-committally. "But I think it was more important to have my facts straight. The professor didn't really care which side of the argument I took, as long as I could back it up." He paused for a second and then added, "Anyway, I really want to go out and celebrate. Why don't you meet me at The Hole in the Wall on Amsterdam Avenue in about an hour, and we'll toast my success?"

Alana frowned slightly. There was nothing she wanted to do more than see Sammy tonight, but it was a Wednesday. "Can't," she told him reluctantly. "It's a school night. You know my folks would freak if I asked to go out tonight."

"Come on, we've snuck out on school

nights before," Sammy reminded her. "Remember last spring when we went to that special *Spider-Man* showing down in the Village?"

Alana giggled, recalling how excited Sammy had been to be one of the first in the city to see Spidey save the world once again. He could be such a kid sometimes.

"Or the time we threw Harrison that surprise birthday party at Hunan Grill?" Sammy continued. "What did you tell your parents that time? That you were at the library?"

"Something like that," Alana admitted.

"So, just tell them you're at Stella's studying tonight."

Alana opened her mouth to protest but stopped herself. She didn't want to make a big thing about this whole "school night" situation. It sounded so totally high school. And Sammy wasn't in high school anymore. He was in a dorm at Columbia—a *coed* dorm, with lots of hot college girls wandering the halls in their bathrobes—or less. Any one of them would be thrilled to help Sammy celebrate his success.

Besides, she wouldn't be completely lying if she told her folks she was studying at Stella's. She was—at the moment anyway. And if she could get through her physics questions in the next hour, she would definitely be entitled to a little fun, wouldn't she? "Yeah, that's a good idea," she said, hoping she didn't sound as reluctant as she felt. "I'll meet you there."

"Can't wait," Sammy told her. "It feels like months since I saw you."

"It was only three weeks ago," Alana replied. "I helped you move into the dorm, remember?"

"I know, but I'm so used to seeing you in school every day."

Alana knew exactly how he felt. This was the first time she'd ever experienced high school without Sammy. Sure, toward the end of last year Sammy had gotten involved in senior activities and all that, so she hadn't seen him as often, but he had still been around, and she never knew when he would suddenly turn a corner or bump into her on the way out of the gym. Now it felt strange to never see him in the halls or on the steps outside the building. That sense of anticipation she got whenever she entered the cafeteria was gone. School without Sammy was definitely not as much fun.

It was good to hear that he felt the same way. Alana had been worried that once Sammy experienced the freedom of dorm life, he'd move on and dump her for someone more . . . well . . . convenient. But that's not what happened at all. She was still the one Sammy called whenever something wonderful happened. Alana smiled. She was his girl, college or not.

"See you in sixty minutes," she told him happily.

"Three thousand six hundred seconds," Sammy replied. "And I'm counting each one."

Alana could feel Stella's eyes on her as she clicked off the phone and tucked it into her pocket.

"*What's* a good idea?" Stella asked her.

"Huh?"

"I said, 'What's a good idea?'" Stella repeated.

"Oh." Alana blushed a little, embarrassed at having to ask her best friend to cover for her. "Um . . . Sammy wants to meet at The Hole in the Wall for a little bit—to celebrate getting a good grade on a paper."

"You're trippin' if you think your 'rents will go for that on a school night," Stella said.

"That's why I need you to cover for me," Alana explained. "They already know I'm here, so I'm just going to let them think we're going to study until eleven. They're both gonna be at the office till at least nine, but if they call . . ."

"I'll tell them you're in the bathroom and then text your cell so you can call them back," Stella said.

"Thanks," Alana replied gratefully. "I would never ask you to do that, except . . ."

"You don't have to give me any reasons," Stella assured her. "What's a best friend for?" She walked over to her closet and pulled out a pale blue tank. "Here, you need to change if you're going to see Sammy."

Alana took the shirt from Stella and held it up in front of the mirror for a look. "It's so soft," she said.

"It's made from hemp," Stella said. "Totally earth friendly material. It takes a lot of pesticides to raise a crop of cotton. But hemp has so few weeds or insects around it, it doesn't need any pesticides at all to grow. That's good for the soil and the atmosphere."

"And it's a cute shirt too," Alana added with a giggle.

"That's what I love most about you," Stella laughed. "You've got your priorities straight."

Alana nodded. And right now her priority was seeing Sammy. "Let's get going on these physics questions," she told Stella. "The sooner I get the homework done, the sooner I can go to The Hole in the Wall."

Two

Alana wasn't sure which felt heavier as she walked up Amsterdam Avenue toward The Hole in the Wall—the hot, sticky, summerlike air or the weight of the guilt she was carrying on her shoulders. The idea of lying to her parents—and, worse yet, making Stella cover for her—was really kind of uncool. In fact, once or twice on her way over to The Hole in the Wall, Alana thought about canceling with Sammy and heading home, but she just couldn't bring herself to do it. She wanted to see him too badly—even if it was just for a little while. Besides, as Sammy had so aptly reminded her, this wasn't the first time she'd done this.

But it was the first time she'd snuck out to meet someone in a *bar*. Alana thought about that for a minute. There were plenty of kids in high school who drank—they had beer parties and all of that. But she and Sammy had never been part of that crowd. This was probably the first time Sammy had ever suggested celebrating success with a drink. Even after his senior prom, Sammy had taken her for a celebratory frozen hot chocolate at Serendipity on the East Side.

Alana sighed. It was a small thing, really. But it was just another sign that she and Sammy were living in different worlds these days. And that seemed to make it all the more important that she meet up with him tonight.

The Hole in the Wall was definitely appropriately named. It was dark and dingy, with sticky, splintered wooden floors and paint peeling from the walls, and the chairs all seemed to have small tears in the leather seats. The whole room smelled sour, like day-old, warm beer. It was hard to imagine anyone hanging out here by choice. But the beer and cheese fries were cheap, which was why so many college kids were there.

Alana wondered nervously if the bouncer

who stood near the front door would throw her out for not having ID. Not that most of the college kids inside were twenty-one either. Still, she wasn't crazy about being somewhere she wasn't really legally allowed to be. Residual effect of having two lawyers for parents, she guessed.

But the bouncer didn't hassle her a bit, and the moment she walked into The Hole in the Wall, Alana knew she'd made the right decision. Sammy was seated at a table off to the side, behind a big pitcher of beer. But he wasn't alone. There was a girl on either side of him. And not just any girls. Hot *college* girls in halter tops and shorts. The sight of Sammy with two girls who may or may not have known that he was taken made Alana feel slightly sick to her stomach.

She glanced in the mirror behind the bar, checking to see if her hair looked okay. A slight curl had begun to form at the bottom, but for the most part, her long, golden brown locks looked nice and straight. It had been hard for her to put her makeup on at Stella's—the glow from the eco-friendly fluorescent lights in her best friend's bedroom hadn't exactly been conducive—but it seemed to have turned out okay. And Alana was glad she'd taken Stella's advice and borrowed the blue hemp shirt. It looked a lot more sophisticated than the Old Navy T-shirt Alana had been wearing, and the pale blue color of the shirt made Alana's blue eyes seem even brighter than usual. Alana may not have been as sophisticated as the scantily clad college girls, but she knew she looked pretty hot.

From the expression on Sammy's face when he spotted her, it was clear he agreed. "'Lana! You made it!" He exclaimed, jumping up from the table and hurrying over to kiss her.

Alana wrinkled her nose a little at the taste of beer on Sammy's lips. She'd never quite gotten the appeal of beer—it tasted kind of sour and just made people act stupid. But Sammy had apparently developed a real liking for it, and he'd been drinking for a while—judging from the sloppiness of the wet kiss he planted on Alana. Not that she minded. Even a wet, sloppy, beer-soaked kiss from Sammy made her feel relaxed and happy.

Sammy wrapped his arm protectively around Alana and turned toward the table of college kids he'd been drinking with.

"Everyone, this is Alana. Alana, this is Diana, Julia, Carlos, Hank, and Paul."

Alana smiled brightly at the table of college kids and tried not to allow her disappointment to show. She'd been hoping this evening would be a private thing—just her and Sammy celebrating the success of the A- paper—but that wasn't what was going on here. This was a group event.

Still, there was a bright side. Sammy wanted her to be part of his new life. Up until now she and Sammy had spent their evenings together either alone or with their old high school buddies. This was the first time Sammy was including her in his college experience. It was nice to know that he wasn't ashamed of having a girlfriend who was still in high school.

"Hey, Alana, grab a seat," one of the girls who had been sitting beside Sammy— "Diana" she thought he'd said her name was—urged. "You want a beer?"

Alana was about to say that her parents would nail her to the floor if she came home with even a hint of beer breath but stopped herself just in time. "No, just a Diet Coke," she said instead. "Trying to watch the calories."

"For what?" Sammy said. "You're perfect."

Alana grinned and kissed him on the nose. "Thanks. I needed that. This was a tough day. The dogs . . ."

"Ooh, you have a dog," Diana squealed. "I miss my little dachshund, Chuckles, so much. What kind of dog do you have?"

"They're not actually *my* dogs," Alana explained. "I'm a dog walker."

"Not professionally," Sammy explained quickly. "Alana's just doing it to earn some bucks."

"I'm saving for college next year," Alana explained. "Tuition at some of the schools I'm applying to is really steep."

"Aren't your parents kicking in?" Julia wondered.

Alana shrugged. "As much as they can. But they're both Legal Aid attorneys. Which means long hours, low pay. Thus, my dog-walking business."

"Too bad they didn't go the *corporate* law route," Paul said. "Then you'd be able to just kick back and enjoy your senior year."

Alana was surprised to hear a friend of Sammy's say something like that. This was definitely a different kind of crowd than he'd hung with in high school. "They're happy. That's what really matters," she said, feeling suddenly defensive. "I'll figure out how to pay for college."

"Where do you want to go?" Carlos asked her.

"Columbia, right babe?" Sammy said, smiling at her with those light brown eyes that made her melt.

"If I can get in. They do have a great social-work school," Alana agreed. "But Hunter does too. And it's a lot cheaper. Or I might want to go out of town to school. I'm not really sure yet."

"You want to be a *social worker?*" Julia asked curiously. "Good luck. It's a tough life. No money in that at all."

"Julia's a business major," Hank explained.

"Don't say it like that," Julia argued playfully. "It's not illegal to want to make a lot of money. I can't help it if I like the good life."

"I guess I just want to make sure *everyone* has a good life," Alana told her. Then, realizing how defensive she sounded, she added, "Actually, I'd like to work as a child advocate some day. I love kids."

"Not me," Julia replied. "I can't stand

them. Have you ever been on an airplane next to a crying baby?"

Alana laughed slightly, hoping Julia was making a joke, but it was hard to tell.

"I think what you want to do sounds great," Diana said, standing up for Alana. "What's a nice girl like you doing with a slug like Sammy?"

Alana smiled. "We have a lot in common," she said. "And besides, he's cute."

Just then a tall, lanky redheaded guy strolled over to the table. "Hey, Sammy, is Tamara here yet?" he asked.

Suddenly everyone at the table got kind of quiet. From their fidgety behavior, Alana figured they weren't too crazy about this guy.

Sammy pulled Alana tighter. "Hi, Joe. I have no idea where Tamara is," he said firmly. "This is Alana. The girl I was telling you about. You know, the one I met in high school."

Joe nodded. "Oh yeah, sure. Hi, Alana. Glad to finally meet you. Sammy talks about you all the time."

Alana smiled. That was good to hear. "Hi, Joe." She wished she could say Sammy had mentioned him as well. But he hadn't.

In fact, up until tonight Sammy hadn't even mentioned any of his college friends.

"You want to sit down and have a drink with us?" Sammy asked, although Alana could tell from the look on his face that he was just trying to be polite.

Joe shook his head. "No. That's okay. I gotta get back to the dorms anyway. Calculus exam tomorrow."

"Oh, that'll be a tough one," Sammy said. "See you later."

As Joe walked off, Sammy turned his attention back to Alana. "So how's it going at old Lincoln High?" he asked her.

"Same old, same old," Alana said. "Christy Shaw is already bossing around all the cheerleaders so badly that half of them want to quit. No shock there, right?"

Sammy nodded. "Did I tell you I heard from Harley?" Sammy asked her. He turned to the other people at the table. "Harley's a friend of mine from high school. He's at Princeton."

"Oooh . . . ," Diana joked. "Princeton. Those tigers think they're all that!"

The other kids at the table laughed.

"A bunch of jocks and legacies," Carlos argued. "Not like Columbia."

Alana sat back and sipped her soda, listening as Sammy and his friends discussed the good and the bad of each of the Ivy League schools. Weird. This wasn't at all what Alana thought college kids would be like. From movies and books and stuff, she'd always figured they sat around talking about intense topics, like what could bring on the end of the world, or whether or not we were really alive—or just the figment of someone else's dreams. *Philosophical* stuff. Or at the very least, whether their football team would kick butt at the homecoming game. But here they were, talking about things like connections, job opportunities, and competing markets. They sounded more like business people having a corporate lunch than college students out for some R&R at a local bar.

Poor Sammy. He must feel so lost in this crowd. He wasn't at all like these people. He was sweet and caring and wanted to help people every bit as much as Alana did. She smiled slightly, remembering how he was the first one to set up a fund-raiser for the victims of Hurricane Katrina and then spent his whole Christmas break down in Mississippi helping to rebuild a school. She reached over and gave him a squeeze and a kiss on the cheek.

"What was that for?" Sammy asked, surprised but not displeased by her sudden show of affection.

"For being you," Alana answered sincerely. "I miss you."

"I'm right here, baby," he assured her.

Alana nuzzled gently against his neck and sighed contentedly. The familiar scent of his cologne was so comforting. Nothing had changed between them—except maybe the few blocks between Lincoln High and Columbia University. Nothing a quick subway ride couldn't correct.

"Hey listen," she said. "The Helping House carnival is next Saturday. I was thinking maybe you'd like to come help out again."

"What's Helping House?" Hank asked.

"It's a kids' charity," Sammy said. "Alana helps out there sometimes."

"Actually, it's for abused moms and their kids," Alana corrected him.

"You sure are into kids," Julia commented.

Alana nodded. "Yeah, I definitely am. Every year they have this massive carnival to

raise money and stuff. I'm going to be volunteering. Maybe you guys would want to
help out."

"Next weekend?" Sammy asked.

Alana nodded. "Yeah."

"That's the big game against Dartmouth,
isn't it?" he asked Hank.

Hank nodded. "You can't miss that,
dude," he said.

Sammy looked over at Alana. "It's a
huge deal when you're in college," he told
her. "Besides, we've got a date *this* weekend.
And I promise I'll meet up with you and
your friends next Saturday night after the
game." He paused for a moment. "You
understand, don't ya, babe?"

Alana didn't completely understand.
You and your friends? They were Sammy's
friends too. Besides, Sammy had never been
particularly into sports before. Still, she
could see where he'd want to fit in at his
new school. And if being at the Columbia-
Dartmouth game could do that for him,
well . . . She nodded slowly. "Sure."

Sammy reached over and gently stroked
her cheek. As he did, Alana caught a
glimpse of the watch on his wrist. *Ten fifteen.*

"Oh, crap!" she blurted out.

"What?" Sammy asked, jumping up, surprised.

The whole table grew silent, staring at her. Alana could feel the embarrassing red blush rushing to her cheeks. "N-nothing," she murmured quietly. "Just that I have to get going."

"Now?" Carlos asked. "Why? Stay a little longer. The night is young."

Alana shook her head. *Not if you have parents at home who think you're studying and will kill you if you get home later than eleven o'clock on a school night,* she thought. But aloud she said only, "Wish I could. But I have a big day tomorrow." *There. That sounded somewhat sophisticated and not too high school. It was pretty much the same excuse that guy Joe had used, and he was in college.*

Sammy nodded understandingly. "I'll walk you out," he said, getting up and taking her by the hand.

"It was nice meeting you all," Alana said, flashing a smile at the group as she followed Sammy out of the bar.

"I wish you could stay," Sammy murmured as they stood together outside on the sidewalk. He wrapped both of his arms around her and pulled her close—so close that Alana could feel his heart pounding next to hers. Alana wasn't usually one for PDA, but tonight she was glad for it. Maybe it was the fact that Sammy had included her in his new life, or maybe it was just that she no longer saw him every day, and therefore every instant was special. Either way, Alana felt no desire to tell him to stop. Instead, she kissed him back, right there, in the middle of Amsterdam Avenue.

Sammy held her tightly, pressing her mouth harder against his own. He tasted like beer, but Alana didn't stop kissing him. In fact, she kissed him harder, refusing to act like a schoolgirl who was repulsed by the slightest taste of alcohol. And in a few seconds the taste of beer seemed to disappear. All she could sense was the nearness of Sammy. Just like always. *And forever.*

"Get a room," a nearby smoker shouted.

The sound of a third party's voice was enough to break the spell that had enveloped Alana. Almost instantly she pulled away; her passion quickly replaced with embarrassment.

"I . . . um . . . ," she murmured helplessly. "It's late. I should go."

"Damn smokers," Sammy grumbled. "Always standing around out here. They should just quit."

Alana smiled despite her embarrassment. That was one argument against smoking that hadn't quite made it to the side of the carton. She could just see it now: "Smoking is hazardous to other people's love lives."

"I really have to get home," she told Sammy quietly.

"I wish you weren't still in high school," Sammy replied.

Alana frowned. There was something in his tone that was incredibly condescending, as though high school were actually kindergarten or something. She had a sudden urge to remind him that just three short months ago he'd been in high school too. But she didn't really want to leave on a bad note. She was afraid to push it. Those girls in there were awfully pretty, and Alana bet there were more where they came from.

"It's almost the weekend," she assured him. "My curfew's one o'clock then." She frowned as the words left her mouth. *Curfew. Oh man, that sounds so babyish.*

"You need me to walk you home?" Sammy asked her.

Alana shook her head. "You go back inside and celebrate that A-, okay? Have one for me."

"You got it," Sammy said. He kissed her quickly and then disappeared back into the crowd of college kids inside The Hole in the Wall.

As Alana headed back toward home, she pulled out her cell phone and hit number three—Stella's speed-dial digit.

"Hey, Alana."

It was such a relief to hear her best friend's voice. "Hey, Stel. Did my 'rents call you?"

"Nope. No one's called all night. You're in the clear."

Well, that's a relief, anyway.

"How was Sammy?"

"Happy," Alana said. "And a little drunk. He was celebrating with his friends when I got there."

"Ooh, college kids," Stella said. "Anyone there I might like?"

Alana considered that for a minute. That Hank kid was kind of cute, but she wasn't sure he was Stella's type. "I don't know.

Next time you'll have to come and pick one out yourself."

Stella laughed. "You make them sound like puppies in a pet-store window."

Alana giggled, suddenly picturing all the kids at the table jumping up and down and banging on the glass, the way the puppies at Puppy Palace did whenever people stopped to peek in.

"So what was it like?" Stella asked her.

"Weird," Alana told her.

"*Sammy* was weird?" Stella wondered.

"No, not Sammy," Alana insisted, although she thought maybe she was trying to convince herself, too. Sammy *had* been acting a little different tonight. But there was nothing she could put her finger on, so she decided to just let it go. "It was his friends. They were a little odd. Not like us, you know?"

"Well, Sammy's new friends are college kids," Stella said. "It's a different kind of life."

Alana sighed. *Sammy's new friends.* She hated how that sounded.

"Did you like them?" Stella asked.

"I think the question is more, did they like me," Alana said. "I was the one being judged tonight. You know, Sammy's high school girlfriend and all that."

"*That* you have nothing to worry about," Stella assured Alana. "There isn't a person in the world who wouldn't like you."

Alana's thoughts shot back to the way everyone at the table grew so quiet and uncomfortable when that Joe guy stopped by. At least they hadn't behaved that way around her. In fact, they'd been perfectly cordial. Maybe Stella was right. Maybe she didn't have anything to worry about at all.

Three

Not that Alana would have had the time to worry, anyway. Her Thursday schedule was insane! The minute school was over, she had to rush over to the El Dorado to pick up Noodles for his afternoon exercise at the dog run in Riverside Park. It would have been so much easier to have taken him to a dog run in Central Park since the El Dorado was right at Ninety-sixth and Central Park West, but Noodles's owner, Mrs. Parker, had made it clear that she wanted Noodles in the dog run at Riverside Park. Apparently another woman in her building had told her it was a much better class of dogs at the Riverside dog run. Far more purebreds.

Alana grinned, remembering Stella's reaction when she'd told her about Mrs. Parker's orders. "Dogs don't care whose butt they're sniffing," Stella had joked at the time. "They all smell the same."

Still, Alana had to do what her customers wanted. And on Thursdays her task was to take Noodles to Riverside Park. So she stopped at the front desk in the big Art Deco lobby of the El Dorado and asked one of the doormen for the key to the Parkers' apartment.

"May I have your name?" the doorman asked.

Alana sighed. She'd been picking Noodles up for his walks for nearly six months now, yet the guards here never seemed to recognize her. "Alana Marks," she replied.

The guard checked his list, nodded, and pulled out the plastic card that passed for a key at the El Dorado. "Please return this—"

"On the way out," Alana finished his sentence with a grin.

For once the doorman grinned back. "Exactly," he said. "Glad you're here. Some of the neighbors have complained that Noodles had been crying at the door this morning. I think he's lonely."

Alana nodded. Of all her clients' dogs, Noodles was the one who most hated being alone. He was always so grateful whenever Alana entered the Parker apartment. So it was no surprise that the bulldog came running as quickly as his chubby little body would allow the minute Alana opened the apartment door. He rubbed against Alana's leg and then looked up at her with a big, goofy smile on his squished-in face.

"You might look scary, but you're just a big mush, aren't you, Noodles?" Alana teased as she bent down and petted his soft, short fur. Noodles gave Alana a good sniff. A second later he opened his mouth and licked her face. Alana laughed, stood up, and turned around slightly before wiping her face with her hand. She wasn't sure dogs could get insulted, but she didn't want to take the chance of letting him know that wet, sticky dog spit wasn't the nicest thing to have all over her face—especially since she knew Noodles's licks were a total act of love and gratitude.

"Okay, Noodles, let's go to the park!"

At the sound of the word "park," Noodles began jumping up and down and barking excitedly. It was a tough job getting his leash on when he was so excited, but somehow, Alana managed to hook it onto the loop around his thick, black leather collar.

A few moments later she and Noodles were outside, on their way to Riverside Park. Noodles walked patiently by Alana's side as they traveled west to Riverside Drive and then headed south to Eighty-seventh Street. He stopped once to sniff the rear end of a shy, chocolate and white springer spaniel, and unfortunately decided to "do his business" right outside a coffee-shop window on Columbus Avenue, but other than that, he was perfectly behaved and completely nonplussed by the hustle and bustle of New York City streets. Maybe that was why Alana felt a real kinship with Noodles and the other dogs she cared for. New York City living, with its stacked apartments, crowded sidewalks, and honking horns, probably wasn't the natural habitat for any animal or person. And yet, it was home. Neither Alana nor her dogs would ever be happy living anywhere else.

The Riverside Park dog run wasn't overly crowded by the time Alana and Noodles arrived. Only a handful of dogs were running around the fenced-in square of sand. Their owners were seated on benches nearby, clutching their cups of Starbucks and gossiping. Alana walked Noodles into the run, locked the gate behind herself, and unhooked his leash. Noodles looked up at her for a moment, unsure.

"Go ahead and play, Noodles," Alana said in her calm, dog-friendly voice. That was all it took. With a loud "woof," Noodles ran off, anxious to sniff any dog he could get near.

As she glanced around the run, Alana had to admit that Mrs. Parker was right to send her all the way to Riverside Park with Noodles. The Eighty-seventh Street dog run was an awfully nice place for a dog to play. For starters, it was really pleasant to be surrounded by the trees and grass of the park. This dog run also had a fountain, so there was always enough cool water for the dogs to drink. And the neighborhood dog owners had installed a hose that squirted long streams of water, which was a great way for the dogs to keep cool—especially on hot days like this. In fact, several of the dog owners were taking advantage of that right now. Alana wiped a couple of beads of sweat from her forehead. It certainly was an unusually warm September day.

Out of the corner of her eye, Alana spotted Leo, a sophomore at NYU who was a dog walker in his spare time, sitting on a bench across the yard, not far from the second, smaller fenced-in area. The one reserved for antisocial dogs. At the moment, the smaller dog run was empty. Alana was glad. She really hated when the dogs in there growled too menacingly or barked too loudly. Alana loved dogs, but even *she* had to admit that some of them could be a little scary sometimes.

"Hi, there," Leo greeted her, moving over to make room for her to have a seat. "You just have Noodles today?"

Alana nodded. "Yeah. And tomorrow I've got all four of them at once. It sort of changes from week to week."

"I have Princess and Morpheus this afternoon," Leo said, pointing to a gray schnauzer and a small, cream-colored pug. "We've been here awhile." He glanced at her face. "You look kinda tired."

"Gee, thanks a lot," Alana joked.

Leo blushed beet red and nervously pushed his black horn-rimmed glasses up on the bridge of his nose. "I didn't mean it in a bad way. I mean, you look really nice, just a little wiped. Like you have something on your mind." He was stepping over his words now, trying to make things right.

With a friendly smile, Alana was able to let Leo off the hook. "I *am* tired," she admitted. "Thanks for asking."

Leo relaxed almost immediately. "So, what's up? You have a heavy date last night or something?"

"Well, yeah, I was out last night, but not late or anything," Alana explained, leaning back on the bench. "I just had a rough day at school. I had a pop quiz in French, and I have a ton of homework waiting for me when I get home. Mostly English and physics."

"I had only one class today," Leo said. "Astronomy. It was pretty far-out."

Alana giggled. "Very *punny*," she teased.

Leo smiled. "I am nothing if not amusing," he said, pulling the brim of his Yankees cap down low over his eyes. "The great thing about college is you mostly take classes you're interested in."

"That would be nice," Alana mused. "The idea of a physics-less college career immediately springs to mind."

"I know what you mean," Leo agreed. "I try to steer clear of the science building as much as possible. Actually, I'm thinking of declaring journalism as my major. That'll mean a lot of writing classes and not so much math and science."

"We are definitely birds of a feather, Leo," Alana told him.

"More like dogs of the same breed," Leo replied with a grin, glancing out into the dog run.

Alana laughed. "Exactly."

Leo leaned back and took a little breath. "You know, I was thinking, if you're not doing anything Saturday night, this band I know is playing at the Knitting Factory—you know, that club in Tribeca. They're really hot. Sort of a mix between grunge and emo. The lead singer is a cross between Kurt Cobain and Eagle-Eye Cherry. And the guitarist totally kicks butt. I kind of produce them, and I could get you in for free."

"You're producing bands now?" Alana was genuinely impressed.

Leo blushed. "Well, not producing exactly. Just setting up their equipment, making sure the soundboard is working right, stuff like that. It's not as glamorous as it sounds."

Alana smiled kindly at him. It didn't actually sound glamorous at all, more like being a glorified roadie or something. But Leo was such a nice guy, she couldn't stand to let him seem uncomfortable about anything. "I think it sounds awesome!" she exclaimed. "And I would love to hear them. I have a thing for Eagle-Eye."

Leo nodded excitedly. "I know. You were telling me that a couple of weeks ago."

"Wow! You have *some* memory," Alana replied. "I can't remember things my teacher told me today."

"It's different," Leo said with a chuckle. "I'm interested in what you have to say."

"As opposed to me and my teachers," Alana added with a laugh.

"Exactly," Leo said. "Anyhow, the show starts at nine. . . ."

"Do you think you could get Sammy in too?" Alana asked. "He's my boyfriend. I think I told you about him. He goes to Columbia. I know he would totally freak to see a band at the Knitting Factory. College students don't have any cash, so he's been kind of deprived in the music department these days."

Leo bit his lip slightly and glanced over to where Morpheus was happily sniffing the butt of a cute little Maltese. "Uh, yeah, Sammy, sure," he said quietly. "Whoever you want."

"Awesome! Thanks!" Alana exclaimed. "This is going to be so great. Finally *I* have plans for us that are mad cool. Usually it's Sammy who comes up with things to do."

"Glad I could help," Leo muttered.

Alana looked at him curiously. Now it was Leo who seemed kind of tired and withdrawn. "You okay?" she asked him.

"Sure, sure," Leo said. "Just keeping an eye on the dogs. You know how nasty Princess can get when someone sniffs her for too long."

"She *is* the definition of bitch," Alana agreed with a grin. "Female dog, right?"

Just then Bridget Mulroney, a heavy-set, middle-aged redhead with a passion for ill-fitting spandex running shorts, came hurrying over to where Alana and Leo were sitting.

"You two aren't going to believe it. I

just found out some amazing news," Bridget told Alana and Leo.

Alana rolled her eyes slightly. Bridget *always* had news. It was rarely amazing. Just gossip from the dog-run set. But for some reason Bridget found the day-to-day relationships between dog owners—or even between the dogs—fascinating. Alana figured it was because she didn't actually work or have kids or anything. The only thing in Bridget's life was her dog, a golden retriever named Goldie (how original!) and a mysterious husband whom no one at the run had ever met.

"Have either of you noticed how Sally Kane hasn't been here the past few weeks?" Bridget asked.

Alana thought about that for a minute. The only person she actually looked for when she brought her dogs to the Riverside run was Leo—he was the only sane person there usually. But now that Bridget brought it up, Alana hadn't seen Sally Kane or her beagle, Persephone, lately.

"Well, I thought Sally had to be on vacation or off showing Persephone," Bridget continued, without waiting for a response from either Alana or Leo. "But it turns out, she's dealing with a major trauma."

Alana sat up straight. A trauma. Now *that* sounded bad. "Is she okay?" she asked Bridget.

"Nothing a little therapy won't help," Bridget assured her.

"What happened to Sally?" Leo asked. He also seemed more curious now.

"Not to Sally. To *Persephone*," Bridget corrected him. "Apparently Sally took her to another dog run—one all the way downtown, where she didn't know the dogs that well. And the next thing Sally knew, Persephone was doing you-know-what with a schnauzer behind a tree!"

Alana struggled to keep from laughing. Leo was not nearly as successful. He burst into absolute hysterics. "I never knew Persephone had it in her," he said between chuckles.

"It's not funny," Bridget told him. "Persephone's pregnant—with mutts!"

"Schnauzer-beagle mixes," Alana mused. "I bet they'll be adorable."

"But Persephone is a show dog. An absolute purebred," Bridget explained, apparently amazed that Alana and Leo were not grasping the seriousness of the situation. "If word gets out in the beagle world that Persephone has been compromised . . ."

"Is that what they're calling it these days?" Leo asked, bursting into a fresh round of laughter. "'Compromised'?" Bridget glared at him.

"Is Sally ever coming back to the dog run?" Alana asked, trying to distract Bridget from Leo's hysterics.

"I don't know," Bridget said. "She's going to have to get all of those puppies adopted before she can show her face again, don't you think?"

"I'm sure she'll have no problem," Alana assured Bridget. "Some people actually prefer mixed breeds. They're usually healthier and smarter."

"I hope you're right, for Sally's sake," Bridget said. "I mean, imagine if she actually had to keep them."

"Imagine!" Leo exclaimed. "The shame of it all."

His sarcasm was totally lost on Bridget. "I know," she agreed. "I feel so awful for Sally. I wish there was something I could do for her. Maybe send a card or something."

"I doubt Hallmark has a card for this

occasion," Leo said, practically choking on his laughter now.

Bridget nodded. "I guess you're right," she agreed, once again missing Leo's sarcasm completely. "It is an unusual occurrence."

"Oh, yeah," Leo said, rolling his eyes. "There are hardly any mutts born in New York."

Bridget didn't reply. Instead, she turned slightly and spotted a man with a large, chocolate Lab entering the dog run. "Oh, there's Joe!" she exclaimed. "I'll bet he hasn't heard about this yet. I'd better tell him."

As soon as Bridget was out of earshot, Alana allowed herself to laugh along with Leo. "I think that was her best story yet," she giggled.

"Oh man, yeah," Leo agreed breathlessly. "That was a classic. Can't you just see the card she'd send? 'So sorry your pup's preggers. Hope you get over your nervous breakdown soon.'"

That did it. Alana was suddenly overcome with a round of unstoppable giggles. "Leo, you're like an island of sanity in a sea of crazies," she said between gasps for air. "I am so glad you're here."

Leo smiled. "Back atcha."

About a half hour later, Leo left the park to take Morpheus and Princess home. Alana didn't really relish the idea of hanging out at the dog run without him, but Noodles was obviously in no mood to move on. At the moment, he was happily chasing a playful pug around the dog run, barking joyfully as he circled the trees and crouched beneath the benches. She couldn't make him leave now, when he was having so much fun and getting the exercise he needed after being cooped up in the apartment all morning.

Noodles was also working up quite a thirst. His tongue was hanging out of the side of his mouth, and he was panting pretty heavily. Eventually the bulldog took a break from his game of chase and hurried over toward the large, metal water bowls that were set up at the edge of the run for just such an occasion. But before Noodles could reach the water, a larger dog ran over to the water bowl and somehow managed to spill its contents all over the surrounding sand and gravel, leaving a yucky brown mud puddle.

"Noodles, no!" Alana shouted as she

watched the bulldog heading toward the mud. "Come! Let's go home!"

But she was too late. Noodles was already rolling around in the mud, joyfully scratching his back in the cool, wet, gravelly mess.

"Your mom is going to kill me!" Alana exclaimed as she went over to the mud puddle and pulled Noodles out. "If you get any of that mud on her white couch . . . well, I wouldn't want to be either one of us." Noodles looked up and gave Alana one of his goofy smiles. "Oh no you don't," Alana scolded him. "You're not going to get away with this that easily. You're going home right now. I'm going to have to give you a bath before your mom gets home!"

Bathing a bulldog was not nearly as easy as it sounded. Sure, Alana had miraculously steered Noodles into the Parkers' bathroom without getting so much as a drop of mud on the furniture, but getting the big guy into the tub was proving to be more of a problem than she'd planned on. It seemed that while Noodles liked mud, he was not nearly as fond of clean water. Forcing a fifty-pound bulldog into a tub was no easy task.

Alana had to crouch down behind Noodles and push on his butt until the unhappy dog finally acquiesced and made the leap into the tub.

Still, once he was in the water, Noodles was a complete angel. "Good dog," Alana praised him as he stood perfectly still and let her scrub his belly. "Good boy, Noodles."

Noodles looked up at her when he heard his name and gave his body a little shake—completely covering Alana with sudsy water.

"Thanks a lot," Alana grumbled. "Now I get to walk through the streets of Manhattan soaking wet." She looked sternly at Noodles. The bulldog looked back at her, and if Alana wasn't mistaken, she was sure she heard him laugh. Or at least make some sort of dog sound that resembled a laugh.

As the dirty water drained out of the tub, Alana grabbed a towel from the bar nearby. Mrs. Parker probably wouldn't like the fact that Alana was using one of her towels to dry the dog, but it was a lot better than leaving a wet Noodles to have free run of the apartment. He'd only wind up drying himself on the rug and leaving the unpleasant odor of wet dog everywhere. Besides, she would put the towel in the hamper before she left. Then the maid who came three times a week would put it in the laundry. Mrs. Parker would never have to touch the dog-tinged towel, ever.

As Alana pulled the towel down and began to rub Noodles's chubby, bulldog body, her eyes fell on something that had been drying on the towel bar—a pair of stretched out, orange and yellow polka-dot, cotton granny panties. "Oh no," Alana groaned, wincing. The last thing she'd wanted to come face-to-face with was Mrs. Parker's underwear. Ugh! TMI!

Mrs. Parker was not a small woman. In fact, she was kind of large and round, with an angry squished-in face. Alana had always thought Noodles was the perfect pet for her, because, physically, Mrs. Parker was pretty much the human version of a bulldog. And the image of her in her bright orange and yellow panties was . . . well . . . Alana blinked hard, trying to get it out of her head.

"Oh, man. You've got to stay out of the mud, Noodles," Alana said as she finally turned the clean, dry bulldog loose into the apartment. "I can't go through this again." She looked back over at the stretched out piece of orange and yellow material on the rack and shivered slightly. Some things were better off unseen.

Four

"It hurts when you walk out the door. I'm not really sure, if I can take much more. . . ." The lead singer's voice leaked out onto the sidewalk as Alana and Sammy approached the Knitting Factory on Saturday night.

"Alana Marks and Sammy Arden," Alana told the bouncer at the door.

The bouncer looked down at the guest list. "I've got Alana Marks and guest. This guy's your guest?"

Alana could feel Sammy bristle at the slight. "Um, yeah," she told the bouncer. "Sammy's my guest."

"Okay," the bouncer said, taking a black marker and drawing lines on Alana's and Sammy's right hands. "Modern Art's playing in the main room. The bar's to your left. You'll need ID for alcohol."

"Thanks," Alana said, flashing a smile at the bouncer as they walked into the club. She turned to Sammy. "This is so cool. I've never been on a guest list at a club before."

"I still haven't," Sammy grumbled, with more than a hint of annoyance in his voice.

"That *was* weird," Alana admitted. "I'm positive I told Leo your name. Maybe he just forgot. Anyway, we're here now. Let's go into the main room. I can't wait to hear Modern Art at full volume."

"Modern Art," Sammy repeated the band's name out loud. "Pretty pretentious name for some college garage band, don't you think?"

Alana shrugged. "I kind of like it. Besides, it's not the name that counts. It's the sound."

"True," Sammy agreed. "Let's give 'em a listen."

As Alana pushed open the door to the main room, she was hit by the sheer blast of Modern Art at full volume. Sure enough, the band was exactly as Leo had promised— emo, with an obvious Nineties grunge influence.

The crowd at the Knitting Factory was very downtown. Nearly everyone was dressed in black—the girls in tight leggings with oversized shirts, the guys in black jeans and retro rock-band T-shirts. Everyone seemed to be pierced, and not always in the obvious places. And tattoos were everywhere. Alana was glad she'd followed Stella's advice and worn a black vest over her long gray shirt and skintight black jeans. She felt as though she really fit in with the ultrahip downtown youth scene.

Unfortunately, Sammy hadn't made as successful a choice in his outfit. He stuck out like a sore thumb in his salmon-colored Le Tigre shirt, khakis, and loafers. It was totally a new look for him. Back in high school he'd been a jeans and T-shirt kind of guy. Still, no matter what he was wearing, Alana thought he was most definitely the hottest guy in the room—close-cropped hair and all. And to prove it, she ran her fingers through that short hair and kissed him on the cheek.

A moment later Leo appeared beside her. Alana jumped with surprise and then grinned. Leo hadn't changed his look for tonight one bit. He was exactly as he had appeared at the dog run—Yankees cap, ripped jeans, and a worn-out, white and purple NYU T-shirt. Like Sammy, he'd made no effort whatsoever to cultivate a downtown sophisticated look. Yet *unlike* Sammy, he seemed to fit in at the Knitting Factory perfectly.

"Alana! I'm so glad you made it!" Leo shouted, straining to be heard over the blaring music. He checked out her attempt at downtown wear. "You look incredible!"

Alana wrinkled her nose and stared at him. "What?" she shouted. "I can't hear you!"

Leo crooked his finger and motioned for Alana and Sammy to follow him back out into the entranceway of the club. As soon as the door closed behind them, they were able to hear one another speak.

"The band's awesome, Leo," Alana told him. "Just like you promised."

"I aim to please," Leo assured her. He held his hand out to Sammy. "I don't think we've met. I'm Leo."

"Sammy," he replied, shaking Leo's hand. "I think Alana mentioned you once or twice. You're a dog walker, right?"

Leo nodded. "Among other things."

"Like producer of this band," Alana

boasted. "And a future Pulitzer prize–winning journalist."

"Let's not go crazy," Leo told her. He smiled, obviously pleased with Alana's show of support. "I haven't even declared a major yet."

"So you're thinking about journalism, huh?" Sammy said. "Columbia's a great school for that."

"So I hear," Leo said. "I'm a sophomore at NYU."

"That's not bad," Sammy replied. He wrapped his arm tightly around Alana's waist. "I think 'Lana here might be considering that as a *safety* school."

"Really?" Leo asked. "You didn't mention that, Alana."

Alana shrugged. "NYU is on my list. But it's no safety school. I don't think there is such a thing anymore."

Leo nodded in agreement. "And man, you'd better be sure when you do choose a school. They're so expensive."

"I had no idea just how expensive until I started looking at schools this summer. They sent the tuition costs with the applications. I've never seen so many zeros in one number." Alana sighed. "That's why my life has gone to the dogs."

"Mine too," Leo said. He held up a fist. "Dog walkers of the world unite!"

Alana grinned and raised a fist in solidarity. "Dog walking is a great part-time job, don't you think? I mean, who wouldn't want to spend afternoons outside playing with dogs? They're so sweet and loving. It's amazing how they make me feel terrific no matter what kind of day I've been having."

"I know what you mean," Leo agreed. "I think they're actually a lot more empathetic than people."

"Exactly," Alana agreed. "I—"

Sammy glanced toward the bar. "You want a drink, Alana?" he asked, interrupting the conversation.

Alana frowned slightly. They had sort of been leaving him out of the conversation. "That'd be great," she said, flashing him a bright smile. "Diet Coke if they've got it. Thanks."

"I'll get it," Leo told her. "They give me sodas for free, since I'm working with the band."

"That's okay," Sammy insisted, stepping to the left to effectively block Leo's path to the bar. "I can afford to buy my girlfriend a Coke."

Leo shrugged. "Whatever you say." He cocked his head slightly to the left, listening. "I gotta go. They're about to finish the set. I've got to go clear the stage and set up for the next one."

As Leo walked away, Sammy shook his head. "Kind of sad," he muttered.

"What is?" Alana asked.

"That kid, Leo. Making such a big deal about being a roadie for some college grunge band."

Alana looked at him strangely. "He's not a roadie. He's a producer, sort of."

"Whatever." Sammy shrugged. "Bet you'll be glad when you've earned enough money for school and you can stop hanging around with people like him."

"What do you mean, 'people like him'?" Alana asked. She was surprised to hear Sammy say anything like that.

"You know, people who float through life with no direction," he explained. "You heard him. He hasn't even declared a major yet."

Alana was really taken aback by his statement. It was so judgmental and completely out of character for Sammy. *What is going on here?*

"So what?" Alana defended Leo. "He's only a sophomore. He's got time."

"If you say so," Sammy said with a shrug. "I'm just glad I know what I'll be studying the next four years though."

"We're lucky. We've always known what we wanted to do," Alana told him. "Leo's got too many interests. He's got to narrow them down."

"Well, I can suggest one interest he can cross off his list," Sammy told her.

"Which?" Alana asked him.

"You," Sammy said firmly. Then, noticing Alana's expression, he added, "Don't tell me you didn't realize he likes you."

"Don't be ridiculous," she insisted. "We're friends. That's all."

"Trust me, Alana, I can tell when someone is interested in my girlfriend. And he definitely is."

Alana frowned. This evening wasn't going the way she'd planned at all. She'd hoped Sammy would like her friend and be happy to go out and listen to music for a change. But instead, here they were, in the entranceway, arguing about the very person who'd gotten them into the club for free.

And arguing was the last thing Alana

wanted to do tonight. Defending Leo any more would only lead to more bickering. "Come on," she said, grabbing Sammy's arm. "I'm here with you tonight. So let's get that soda and get in there before the set ends!" And with that, she pulled Sammy back into the main room, where the music was so loud, they couldn't argue even if they wanted to.

"I'm telling you, Stella, it was bizarre," Alana said the next morning as she and her best friend wandered in and out of the narrow aisles of the flea market on Columbus Avenue. "He actually seemed jealous of Leo."

Stella held a vintage white blouse up to her chest and glanced in the nearby mirror. "You know, it's possible he's worried that you're making a whole life for yourself that doesn't include him," she suggested as she studied her reflection. "Up until now he's seen you at school every day. You had all the same friends—well *almost* all."

Alana frowned. She knew what Stella meant by that. Stella and Sammy had never been close. They were just too different. But for Alana's sake, they'd always been cordial enough when they were all together. Stella was obviously glad to have Sammy taken out of the equation when the girls went to school events and stuff together. For that matter, Sammy didn't seem to miss hanging out with Stella, either.

Stella shook her head and put the shirt back in the five-dollar bargain bin at the flea-market stand. "He's just all weirded out that you have friends he's never met before," she told Alana. "He'll get used to it."

Alana sighed. She wasn't so sure about that. After all, she hadn't completely gotten used to the fact that Sammy had new friends that she didn't know. Friends who were influencing the way he dressed and thought. Friends who were girls. Girls without curfews. She blinked her eyes tightly, as though trying to banish the chain of negative thoughts from her head.

"Do you think this is me?" Stella asked, holding up a gauzy pink top with macramé trim.

"Totally," Alana said. "It would look great with your faded Levi's."

"That's what I was thinking," Stella agreed. She flipped her long red curls over her shoulder and reached into her huge pocketbook for a five-dollar bill.

"You need a bag?" the man who owned the flea-market stand asked her.

Alana grimaced. This wasn't going to be pretty.

"No, I don't need a bag," Stella told him. "Do you know how long it will take the plastic from those bags to break down? Hundreds of years. And when they do, they leak all kinds of chemicals into the soil and the water. Poisonous chemicals! And that's only the ones that break down. How about all the bags that get into the ocean and kill off fish and dolphins?" She pointed to the pile of plastic bags on the pavement. "Those are weapons of mass destruction!" Stella declared.

Alana had to choke back a laugh. The owner of the clothing stand looked positively petrified. The people in the nearby stands didn't look too comfortable either. One of them threw her coat over her pile of plastic bags in an effort to conceal her "weapons" from Stella's eyes.

"I'll just put the shirt in my bag," Stella continued, tucking the shirt into her giant pocketbook. "A *cloth* bag, not leather. No animals had to die for this to be made."

As Stella stormed off, Alana glanced

back and gave the owner of the clothing stand a weak smile. She felt kind of bad for him. He'd been just standing there minding his own business, and—*boom*—he'd been attacked by Stella, the guerrilla environmentalist. It had to have been scary for him.

"You think he learned anything?" Stella asked Alana a few moments later.

"Sure," Alana told her. "I'm sure he'll switch to paper bags from now on."

Stella's hazel eyes glared at her. "Paper? He can't use paper! Do you know how many rain-forest trees are cut down each year so we can have paper bags?" She turned back toward the clothing stand.

But Alana grabbed her arm before she could head back for another attack. "I think he's learned enough for one day," she told Stella. "Let's go get some ice cream."

"Cold Stone vanilla with Heath bars mixed in?"

Alana nodded. "Absolutely."

"Sounds perfect," Stella agreed.

Alana grinned. Nothing like Cold Stone ice cream to chill Stella out. That was one problem solved. Now, if only her worries about Sammy could be fixed so easily.

Five

It was impossible for Alana to get Sammy out of her head. All through the school day she was checking her cell phone, hoping for a message from him. No dice. She comforted herself by reminding herself that he had three classes on Monday. Still, how long could it take to just text her a quick "**<3 ya**"? If Sammy were still at Lincoln High, she could have at least caught a glimpse of his soft brown eyes and gotten some reassurance that everything was all right. Of course, if he were still at Lincoln, none of this would be happening. Alana couldn't help but notice that the thirty-block distance between Lincoln High and Columbia University was seeming farther and farther every day.

When the school day ended, Alana was actually glad that she had a whole afternoon of dog walking ahead of her. Mrs. Stanhope had paid her extra to give Nicolette a good workout in the park, which meant that Alana could go for a run around the reservoir with the poodle beside her. It was the perfect afternoon activity. "Nothing like a good endorphin surge to make a girl feel better," she murmured as she laced up her running shoes and headed over to the Stanhope apartment.

The Stanhopes lived in the Beresford apartment building on Central Park West. It was one of those massive, old, prewar buildings that boasted gorgeous views of Central Park and plenty of celebrity residents. Not that Alana had ever seen any of them.

Or if she had, she hadn't recognized them. Alana wasn't very good at spotting celebs. That was Stella's big talent. On one afternoon Stella had seen Madonna, Woody Allen, and Leonardo DiCaprio. Alana hadn't recognized any of them. So it was possible that Alana had seen comedian Jerry Seinfeld or tennis legend John McEnroe in the elevator at the Beresford and just not realized it.

Then again she might have seen Mr. or Mrs. Stanhope in the lobby of the building and not recognized them, either. Alana had only seen one photo of them around the apartment—their wedding portrait. And after twenty-five or so years of marriage, she doubted they still looked the same.

It was strange that Alana had never actually come face-to-face with any of the Stanhopes. Usually the dog owners she worked for liked to sit down and meet with her to watch how she interacted with their dogs. But Mrs. Stanhope had done the whole interview over the phone and hired Alana on the spot. From then on they'd only communicated through notes and pay envelopes tacked to the big bulletin board in the Stanhopes' kitchen.

From their short conversations, Alana had learned that the family needed a dog walker because Mrs. Stanhope spent most of her time at meetings for various committees around the city, and Mr. Stanhope was often away on business trips. Apparently, when their daughter Catherine lived at home, she'd walked Nicolette during the day. And when she'd left for Yale, someone else had taken over the job. But now the person who'd been Nicolette's dog walker was no longer available. Mrs. Stanhope hadn't given any details. All Alana knew was that now Nicolette was alone most days, which was why the family needed a dog walker. Frankly, Alana wondered why the Stanhopes needed a *dog*, since they obviously weren't around enough to enjoy Nicolette. But Alana would never say something like that to Mrs. Stanhope. It wasn't her place to tell people how to take care of their pets. And besides, if it weren't for people like the Stanhopes, she wouldn't have a job.

While she might not have recognized the two elder Stanhopes, Alana would have been able to spot Catherine anywhere. The Stanhopes had practically papered the walls with photos of their soccer-playing daughter. Everywhere Alana went in the apartment, she saw photos of the twenty-year-old: There were photographs of Catherine's graduation from a ritzy Upper East Side girls school, snapshots of her holding trophies and playing soccer with the West Side Soccer League, even pictures of her as a baby kissing a life-size Elmo at Sesame Place in Pennsylvania. And of course, there were plenty of pictures of her smiling in front of the buildings of

Yale University, where she'd been for the past two years. Mrs. Stanhope had made a point of mentioning that with pride several times during their phone conversation. Although she'd never met the girl, Alana felt like she knew Catherine's whole life story.

That was what was so weird about being a dog walker. Since Alana had unrestricted access to her clients' homes, she knew a lot about their lives, while they knew almost nothing about hers. But trophies and photos of a daughter away at college were the most benign of the clues to the secret lives of her clients that Alana came across on a daily basis. The calendars on the wall let Alana know just where her customers were at any given point during the day. The dishes left in the sink clued her in on just who was cheating on their diets. And as she'd already discovered at the Parkers, the things she saw in their bathrooms gave away more secrets than Alana wanted to think about.

Alana never told anyone about the things she discovered in her dogs' apartments though. She figured the secrets she knew about her clients were covered by some sort of dog walker–client privilege. These people were giving her permission to enter their apartments when no one was home. That came with a real responsibility. Discretion was a major part of the dog-walker's job description.

In the three months since she had been working for the Stanhopes, no one—not even the maid—had ever been in the apartment at the same time Alana was. So she was really surprised to hear a banging noise coming from the living room as she entered the apartment.

"Hello," Alana called out nervously as she cautiously entered the apartment.

Nicolette came running at the sound of Alana's voice.

"Good girl," Alana said, bending down to pet the excited poodle. "You sure are happy today. Are Mommy and Daddy home with you?"

But it certainly wasn't Mr. or Mrs. Stanhope who suddenly emerged from the living room. Not unless Mr. Stanhope was about eighteen years old or so, because the guy Alana was facing couldn't be much more than that.

Whoever this fellow was, he was certainly comfortable in the Stanhope apartment. He was walking around bare-chested, wearing nothing more than a pair of faded jeans and a tan leather tool belt. He was also probably the most gorgeous example of man Alana had ever seen.

"Hello," Alana said, forcing herself to shift her eyes from his incredibly sculpted six-pack abs to his face so she could actually get up the courage to speak to him. But the change of focus was no help, since his deep-set, chocolate brown eyes were every bit as disarming as his abs. "I'm Alana, the dog walker."

"Connor," the hottie replied. He placed his hammer back into his tool belt and held out his hand for her to shake.

"I didn't know anybody would be here," Alana said weakly, nearly melting at the touch of his hand. *Man, this guy is so amazing looking. Like something out of an A&F catalog.*

"I just stopped by to fix the curtain rod in the living room," Connor explained, running his hands through his shoulder-length brown hair.

That explains what he is doing in the apartment. He's the building superintendent or handyman or something. "You did a good job," she complimented him, not sure of what to say. "The curtains look straight."

"I can be a perfectionist when I need to be." Connor flashed her a grin. "I've never seen you here before. Do you walk Nicolette every day?"

Alana shook her head. "Mondays, Wednesdays, and Fridays. Those are the days Mrs. Stanhope has her meetings."

"Oh yes, those *society* meetings," Connor said in a sarcastically snooty voice. "Very important."

Alana laughed. This whole thing was like something out of a British independent film. She and Connor were the hired help, working while the society folks were out doing whatever it was rich people did during the day. Connor was the hottie handyman, while she was the . . . Alana glanced down at her old, black running shorts and the tie-dyed T-shirt she'd made at camp three summers ago. *Oh great. What a day to be dressed like a slob!*

"I . . . uh . . . I'd better go check the bulletin board and see if Mrs. Stanhope has left me any instructions for Nicolette," Alana said.

"She leaves you notes instead of calling you?" Connor asked.

Alana nodded.

"That doesn't insult you?"

"No. It's easier that way."

"I'm sure," Connor replied with a laugh.

"Do you know the Stanhopes?" Alana asked him.

Connor nodded. "Sure. But we mostly communicate through notes too."

Alana could feel her heart pounding slightly as he spoke, and she suddenly caught herself staring at his abs again. Her cheeks began to feel all hot; she was certain Connor could tell she was blushing. "Well, um . . . it was nice meeting you," she murmured. "I . . . um . . . really should get started with Nicolette."

As Alana hurried into the kitchen to check the bulletin board, an overwhelming feeling of guilt washed over her. What was she doing staring at Connor that way? She had a boyfriend. A guy she really liked. She wasn't supposed to be staring at someone else's abs or admiring the way his eyes were so dark brown they looked like chocolate cupcakes floating in a sea of white cream.

Yikes! She really had been studying him. This was not good.

Come on, Alana, chill out, she told herself silently. *You aren't doing anything wrong. A girl can look at the menu all she wants, as long as she doesn't order anything.*

Yet somehow she knew Sammy wouldn't see it that way. He'd gotten so mad over Leo, and Alana wasn't attracted to him at all. Not that she was attracted to Connor or anything. That would be impossible. After all, they'd only spoken a few words to each other.

And Alana was going to keep it that way. She hurried into the kitchen and immediately busied herself, getting Nicolette's portable, collapsible water bowl from the cabinet and grabbing a bottle of water from the fridge. The sooner she got out of there, the better.

"Thirsty?" Connor asked in his deep, friendly voice.

Alana whipped around and once again came face-to-face with those brown eyes. "No," she said quickly, trying to look away. "I mean, it's not for me. These are Nicolette's water bottles. Mrs. Stanhope wants her to have only bottled water."

Connor rolled his eyes. "She's a dog."

"I know," Alana said. "But she's *Mrs. Stanhope's* dog. I do what she tells me to do for her." She glanced up at the bulletin board. "Oh, man," she groaned.

"What?"

"Mrs. Stanhope says there's a steak in the refrigerator for Nicolette. She wants me to cut it into bite-size pieces for her after we get back from the park." Alana sighed heavily. "I swear, with the money that steak cost, they could probably feed four homeless families and . . ." She stopped herself midsentence and looked down at the floor. She really wasn't in the habit of complaining about her clients to people she didn't know. But for some reason, she sensed Connor would understand what she meant. After all, Connor was the handyman in a building full of wealthy people. He probably dealt with plenty of folks who squandered their money the way the Stanhopes did.

"These people definitely have weird priorities," Connor agreed, as if confirming what Alana was thinking. He grabbed an orange from a nearby bowl of fruit and slowly began tearing away the peel. "So what do you do when you're not working for Mrs. Stanhope?"

Alana looked at him with surprise. She would never have taken anything to eat or drink from any of her clients' apartments.

But Connor had made himself completely at home in the kitchen.

"I . . . uh . . . I'm a senior, at Lincoln High. And sometimes on weekends I volunteer at Helping House . . . ," Alana muttered nervously. *What is it about this guy that makes me so tense, anyway?*

"Helping House?" Connor asked.

"It's a place for women and kids who have been abused. They help them get back on their feet. I spent a lot of time there over the summer but not so much now. Although this Saturday afternoon I'm going to go over and help with their carnival. It's a big fundraiser. There are rides and snacks and old-fashioned carnival games, like a dunking booth and stuff."

Connor grinned. "That was always my favorite as a kid. Especially if I could make sure my teachers got dunked."

"I know what you mean," Alana said, returning his grin. Then she caught herself staring into his eyes again. "Anyhow," she continued, forcing herself to look away, "school takes up a lot of my time. And then there's all the dog walking. I need to do that, though, if I'm going to pay for college next year." Alana frowned and struggled to stop herself from talking. She was definitely jabbering on too much.

But Connor didn't seem to mind. He just sat there, listening to her every word, his eyes never leaving hers. They were practically burning right through her.

"So . . . um . . . I'd better run," Alana said, heading back toward the front hall where Nicolette's leash was kept.

Connor followed close behind. So close that Alana could practically feel him. "Do you ever have time in that busy schedule to go out—like to a movie or dinner or something?" he asked her.

Alana turned to look at him. Her heart was beating really hard now. "No," she said quickly. *Too quickly.* "I mean, I sort of have a boyfriend."

"Sort of?" Connor asked, his eyes twinkling.

"No. I mean, not *sort of* . . . Definitely. I have a boyfriend," Alana jabbered helplessly, unable to control her own mouth. "His name's Sammy."

"Oh," Connor said. He shoved his hands into his pockets and shrugged. "Well, lucky Sammy. My loss. Have a good run with Nicolette."

"Thanks," Alana replied. She hurried out the door with Nicolette by her side. She pushed the button for the elevator and stood there, fully aware that Connor had not shut the apartment door and was staring at her from down the hall.

"Well, that was a disaster," Alana told Nicolette as she stepped into the elevator and watched the steel door slide shut. "I made a complete jerk out of myself. Good thing I'll never see him again."

The poodle looked up at Alana and barked.

But Alana did see Connor again. The minute Alana entered the apartment on Wednesday afternoon, he walked out of a back bedroom, with Nicolette happily nipping at his heels. This time he was wearing jeans and a black T-shirt with the logo of *Rolling Stone* magazine emblazoned on the front. Alana was glad for the T-shirt. The sight of a bare-chested Connor and those amazing abs was really just too much for her to handle.

"Hi, Alana."

"You're back again." Alana frowned as the words exited her mouth. *Of course he's back again, you jerk. He's standing right there.*

Luckily, Connor didn't seem to notice the obviousness of Alana's statement. "I was just fixing something in the—um—spare bedroom," he told her. "You and Nicolette going for a run today?"

Alana shook her head. "Just a regular walk. But I'm taking four dogs."

"All at once?" Connor asked, sounding impressed.

"Yep," Alana told him. "It's not that bad—unless one of them spots a squirrel."

Connor chuckled. "I can see where that might be a problem."

"You have no idea," Alana agreed. She bent down and petted Nicolette. "How are you, pretty girl?" she cooed, using the dog as an excuse not to stare into Connor's eyes any longer. She wasn't sure what it was about this guy that made her feel so guilty. It wasn't like she was even flirting with him or anything. Or like he was flirting with her. He was just working. Same as she was.

"I'd better go check the board for instructions," Alana said, heading into the kitchen.

"Maybe Mrs. Stanhope wants you to pre-pare pheasant under glass for her precious pup," Connor joked.

"Nope," Alana replied with a laugh. "Too many small bones." She looked at the note on the board. "Actually, Nicolette's getting dog food today. A new recipe from the Barkery."

"The what?"

"The Barkery," Alana repeated. "It's a dog supermarket on Columbus Avenue."

"You mean a pet shop?"

Alana shook her head. "Not exactly. This place bakes its own treats and grinds its own meat."

Connor rolled his eyes. "And it costs a fortune, right?"

"Yep," Alana said.

"The Stanhopes are amazing," Connor said. "I don't get it. I never have."

"Me either," Alana agreed. "But I try not to judge." That wasn't exactly true. She judged all the time. She just would never do so out loud.

Alana moved toward the edge of the kitchen, squeezing past Connor to get to the hallway for Nicolette's leash. The proximity of his body to hers sent a flash of heat through her limbs. She hoped she wasn't blushing too hard.

"You want company on your walk?" Connor asked her.

Alana wanted to say no. She knew she *should* say no. But the only word that came out of her mouth was "sure."

Connor flashed her a big smile. "Great!" he exclaimed, sounding as happy as a three-year-old who'd just been offered a ride on the carousel in Central Park. "I really need to get out of here for a little while."

"You're incredibly good with dogs," Alana complimented Connor a little while later as they walked through the Ramble with Nicolette, Noodles, Frisky, and Curly. "Especially Nicolette. She's usually skittish around strangers, but she's acting like she's known you her whole life."

"Animals like me," Connor said. "I don't know why."

"My dad says you can tell what kind of person someone is by the way he gets along with animals," Alana remarked. "They're true judges of character."

Connor flashed her another of his disarming grins. "So I guess that means I'm okay."

Much better than okay, Alana thought as once again she struggled to keep her breathing in check while she was in Connor's presence. After a beat she said simply, "Yeah, that's what it means."

They walked along in silence for a little while enjoying the quiet of the woods and each other's company. After a while, they reached a brown, wooden pagoda that was hidden away among some trees. "You want to sit down for a while?" Connor asked.

"Sure," Alana agreed, following him to the bench. For once the dogs cooperated, lying down in a row at their feet. "They're tired," she remarked. "Even Frisky, which is unusual. He's usually bouncing all around. But look at him—he's just lying there, totally fried."

"Mmhmm," Connor replied. "I am too. The heat can take it out of you."

"Your work is pretty physical too," Alana reminded him.

"My *work*?"

"Yeah, you know, fixing things at Beresford. That must be hard work."

"I've always been good at fixing things," Connor replied nonchalantly. "But my real career is as a photographer. I've been putting together a portfolio."

Alana was genuinely impressed. "I had no idea you were an artist."

Connor smiled. "You don't know a whole lot about me," he reminded Alana.

She blushed slightly. That was true. "So tell me about yourself. What kind of photography do you do?"

"Candids mostly. People just being people. I think those are the most interesting kinds of photos." His whole face lit up as he spoke about his photographs. "Like there's this one I took in Coney Island last summer. I spotted this old couple, all dressed up, walking on the boardwalk. She was in this lacy dress, and he was actually wearing a sport jacket—in the middle of the summer. They looked so out of place among all the people in their bathing suits and shorts. Like they were from a completely different time or place. But they were the most romantic people I'd ever seen. They were holding hands and smiling at each other. And I just pulled out my camera and captured the moment."

"That sounds beautiful," Alana said. "I'd love to see it."

Connor grinned mischievously. "You want to come up to my place and look at my pictures?" he teased.

Alana blushed slightly, but she felt far

less self-conscious around Connor than she had back at the apartment. In the past hour he'd become less of a modern day, New York version of a Greek god and more of a person. An incredibly good-looking person, for sure, but a person just the same. "Maybe another time," she replied finally.

"I'm gonna hold you to that," Connor told her.

"No, seriously," Alana said. "I really want to see your work some time."

"But that's all you're interested in, huh?" Connor asked more seriously.

Alana kicked at the dirt below her feet. "Connor, I told you. I have . . ."

"I know, you have a boyfriend," Connor said. "I hope he knows how lucky he is."

Alana smiled. "I think he does." *At least I hope he does,* she thought silently, recalling that Sammy still hadn't called her this week. Of course, he was busy. Columbia had to be really tough. Much tougher than high school. He was probably studying right this second while she was out here relaxing with the dogs in the park. Make that with the dogs *and Connor*. A fresh wave of guilt washed over her.

"So are you and Sammy getting together

this weekend?" Connor asked in a voice that was clearly meant to sound nonchalant, but didn't.

"Yeah, we're supposed to . . ." She sat up excitedly. "Ooh! You should come!"

"On a date with you and Sammy? I don't think so."

"No. It's totally not a date. It's just a whole bunch of us getting together at Pomodoro Pizza on Saturday night," Alana assured him.

"That huge pizzeria in the village?" Connor asked. "It's right near my apartment."

"Oh, wow. You live in the coolest neighborhood," Alana said enviously. "Anyway, it's going to be a huge group of people. You'd really like them."

"Even Sammy?" Connor asked, only half teasing.

"Oh, you'll like him. Everyone does," Alana said. "He's just like you and me. Really mellow and laid-back. And he cares about the same sort of things we do, like animals and the arts and kids' rights. He's a major humanitarian."

Connor nodded slowly, but he didn't say a word.

"And I can't wait for you to meet my best friend, Stella," Alana continued. "She's gorgeous. And really smart."

Connor eyed her curiously. "This wouldn't be a setup, would it?"

"No. Honest," Alana said, although she was obviously being less than truthful, and they both knew it. But from Alana's point of view, having Connor hook up with Stella would be awesome. Ever since Stella had split up with Frank Lorimer back in the beginning of junior year, she'd been totally single. No one had really interested her. And she'd gotten into a real man-hating sort of phase. But there was no way Stella wouldn't find a guy like Connor intriguing. There was no way *anyone* wouldn't.

"What time are you going to be there?" Connor asked.

"Around eight. I need time to wash up and stuff after I work at the carnival."

"I'll try to drop by," Connor said.

"That'd be so great," Alana told him sincerely. She glanced down at her watch and leaped to her feet. "Oh man, we'd better get going. I have to get Frisky to a pedicure appointment."

Connor started laughing. "Only in New York," he declared.

"Exactly," Alana agreed as she began to lead the dogs out of the Ramble toward Central Park West. As she walked, a smile of satisfaction flashed across her face. She was really happy Connor would be coming to Pomodoro Pizza on Saturday. He was so incredibly perfect . . . for *Stella*, that is.

Six

"I'm telling you, Stella, you're going to love Connor," Alana promised her best friend as the girls climbed the stairs of the subway stop at Astor Place in the East Village on Saturday night. "He's really nice, and smart. And he's gorgeous."

Stella giggled. "Yeah, you mentioned that," she said. "A few times. In fact, all you've been talking about today is this guy."

"That's because he's so amazing," Alana replied.

Stella looked at her dubiously. "I hate fix-ups," she groaned.

"You don't have to marry the guy. Just give him a chance." Alana paused for a second. "It's been a long time, Stella."

"Yeah, well, I'm gonna be pickier from now on," Stella explained. "I was burned pretty badly last year. I'm not going through that again."

"I can't imagine Connor burning anyone," Alana assured her. "He's too nice. And he's very honest. Not at all like Frank."

Stella bristled slightly at the very mention of her ex's name. "I don't know, 'Lan. According to you, this Connor guy is gorgeous, honest, nice, artistic, athletic . . . nobody can be that perfect."

"Oh, he is. Connor is perfect. . . ." Alana insisted. "For *you*," she added quickly. Maybe *too* quickly.

"Uh-huh," Stella replied suspiciously. "Speaking of men, what time is College Boy showing up tonight?"

Alana shot Stella a glance. "Could you try to be nice to him tonight?" she pleaded. "He's been under a lot of pressure. He hasn't even been able to get the time to call me. I didn't talk to him all week. I finally reached him this morning before he went to the Columbia-Dartmouth game. He said he was at his desk—he had fallen asleep while he was studying."

"I'm always nice," Stella assured Alana.

"It's Sammy that has a problem with me. And I can't imagine why."

"Maybe it's because you called him a murderer at the Spirit Week pep rally last year?" Alana suggested.

"Well, what do you call someone who kills dolphins and seals?" Stella asked her.

"You don't know that the balloons he released into the air ever killed any animal."

"And you can't say that they didn't," Stella argued. "You know as well as I do that those balloons had to come down somewhere. Most of them wind up in the water. And then fish or other wildlife swallow them and suffocate."

Alana sighed. She knew better than to argue with Stella about environmental issues. She glanced at her reflection in a nearby shop window. "Does my hair look okay?"

Stella nodded. "It looks fine. So does your makeup. *And* your outfit. You've already asked me this five times. I don't know what the big deal is. It's just Pomodoro Pizza, not Tavern on the Green."

"I just want to look good; is that a crime?" Alana replied defensively.

"No," Stella said. "It's just weird for you."

Alana didn't know how to answer that. Until recently she hadn't been obsessed with her appearance. But now that Sammy was at Columbia and she'd met Connor . . . Alana blinked her eyes and tried to imagine a big, red stop sign in her brain. She refused to let herself think about Connor at all, unless it was in terms of getting him together with Stella.

"Here we are," Stella said as the girls approached the pizza place. She opened the door and walked inside. "Everyone's at that big table in the back."

Well, not everyone. As Alana walked toward the rear of the restaurant, she was painfully aware that neither Sammy nor Connor were seated in the crowd. In a strange way, that seemed to relax her. The pressure was off—although she wasn't quite sure exactly what was making her feel pressured.

"Uh-oh! Hide the paper napkins; the Queen of Green has arrived," Evan Canter, one of Stella and Alana's classmates, teased as the girls grabbed seats at the end of the table.

"You know it," Stella replied with a grin. "I hope you didn't drive that heap of junk you call a car here tonight."

"Nope. Took the subway," Evan said. "Gas's three bucks a gallon. I'm not driving any more than I have to."

"Speaking of gas . . . you guys want pepperoni on the next pie?" Zach Richter, another Lincoln High senior, asked.

"Funny," Evan said.

"Nothing like a little fart humor to make a night out a success," Zach joked.

"Can we get meatballs on half?" Jessica Kauffman, Zach's girlfriend, wondered.

"Fine with me," Alana said. "Anything but onions."

"Oooh, Sammy must be coming tonight," Evan teased. "Gotta keep your breath fresh."

Alana blushed. He'd read her mind.

"Where *is* Sammy, anyway?" Jessica asked Alana. "I figured he'd be arriving with you."

"He'll be here later. He had some last-minute things to finish up at the dorm," Alana explained. "And I invited another friend to come along. His name's Connor. He should be here any minute."

"Is he cute?" Rebecca Fieldston, a tall, dark-haired girl who'd graduated with Sammy, asked.

"What, you've already gone through all the guys at City College?" Zach asked her.

Rebecca rolled her eyes and blatantly ignored him.

"Connor's unbelievably cute," Stella told Rebecca.

"You've met him?" Rebecca asked her.

Stella shook her head. "Nope. That's just what Alana's been telling me all day."

"Does Sammy know you've been making friends with cute guys?" Evan asked Alana.

Alana frowned. Sammy didn't know about Connor. But then again, there was nothing for him to know. She and Connor were just friends. Just like the girls in Sammy's dorms were *his* new friends. Although Alana hoped girls like Diana and Julia—the girls she'd met at The Hole in the Wall the other night—weren't popping up in his dreams the way Connor kept suddenly showing up in hers. Not that she would've ever told anyone about that!

"I need a Diet Coke," Alana said, changing the subject. "Immediately. I'm fried. I was on my feet all day."

"Doing what?" Jessica asked.

"It was carnival day at Helping House," Alana said. "I was working with the kids at the pie-toss booth."

"They're lucky to have you," Stella told her.

Alana flashed a grin at her best friend. "I'm lucky to have them too. They're great kids. And it's nice to be appreciated once in a while."

"Awww, we appreciate you," Evan teased. "Like we'll appreciate it when you chip in on the bill at the end of the night."

"Gee, thanks a lot, pal," Alana joked back.

"Hey, check it out, Sam the Man's here!" Rebecca cheered, pointing toward the door. "What the heck's he wearing?"

Alana looked over toward the entranceway. Sammy looked more like he had the night at the Knitting Factory than like he had looked when he was in high school. She figured this was his new style. Still, it seemed a little weird—like he was trying to set himself apart from his old pals. After all, he knew he was going to be hanging out in the East Village with their old, high school crowd. Jeans, sneaks, and a T-shirt would have been just fine. But Sammy had arrived in a pair of khaki chinos, a pale blue button-down shirt, and new tan loafers.

"Whoa, dude's gone all preppy on us," Evan remarked.

"I think he looks adorable," Alana said, getting up and hurrying over to greet her boyfriend. "Hi, handsome."

Sammy gave her a grin. "You don't look so bad yourself." He took her hand and gave her a soft, quick kiss on the lips.

Alana looked at him curiously. Funny, the kiss didn't seem as intense or sincere as usual. Maybe Sammy was just tired.

"So how's life up at One Hundred and Sixteenth Street?" Zach asked Sammy.

"Amazing," Sammy told him as he grabbed a seat. "Great people. I'm making incredible connections."

Now it was Stella's turn to give Sammy an odd look. "Connections?" she asked him. "Is that college slang for friends?"

Alana gave Stella a swift kick under the table.

"Ouch!" Stella exclaimed. "What was that for?"

"I've got plenty of friends," Sammy told Stella as he looked out over a whole table of them. "I'm not in college to become popular. I'm there to get my career going. And I'm definitely on the right track. In fact, I start my new internship next week!"

"Oh, wow!" Alana squealed. "An internship? Already? I thought Amnesty International didn't take kids until they'd been in school at least a year."

"Oh, it's not with Amnesty International," Sammy said.

"But that's where you said you were going to apply next year. I thought you figured that as a poli-sci major, you'd be able to—" Alana began.

"I switched majors," Sammy told her.

"In one week?" Alana asked, her voice scaling up slightly.

"I've been thinking about it for a few weeks, actually," Sammy said.

"But at the Knitting Factory you were all over Leo about not having chosen a definite major yet," Alana recalled.

"He's a sophomore," Sammy told her dismissively. "By now he should have a game plan. I'm just a freshman, and now I'm on track for my business degree."

"B-business?" Alana asked. She was stunned.

Sammy nodded proudly. "And yesterday I got the news that my application for an internship at Shoreman Sporting Goods corporate offices was accepted. Now, it's just a nonpaying internship in their marketing department but—"

"Of course it's nonpaying," Stella told him. "Shoreman's not exactly known for paying its workers."

Alana knew what Stella meant. Just last year there had been a whole series of articles in the *New York Times* about Shoreman Sporting Goods using child labor in foreign sweatshops to make their sneakers. The concept of Sammy—*her Sammy*—working for a company like that just didn't compute. Sammy cared too much about people to ever work for a corporation like Shoreman. This had to be a joke.

"Those articles in the *New York Times* were filled with lies and innuendos," Sammy told Stella. "Honestly, I don't know how you believe that crap. The *Times* isn't worth the paper it's printed on."

"I agree," Stella said. She laughed at Sammy's stunned reaction. "But I don't read the actual news*paper*. I read it online. That way no trees have to be cut down for me to get my news."

Alana tried to listen as her best friend and her boyfriend bickered back and forth, but she was lost in a haze. Things were all topsy-turvy. It was like she'd entered some alternate universe where up was down and black was white.

"Why didn't you tell me about this yesterday?" Alana finally managed to murmur.

"I guess I heard about it and just ran out to celebrate," Sammy explained with a shrug. "But I'm telling you now. Proud of me?"

Alana didn't know how to answer that. Proud? That Sammy was working for a company that supported—or at the very least was *rumored* to support—child labor? How could she be? But Sammy was sitting there with such a joyous grin on his face that Alana couldn't bear to argue with him. "If you're happy, I'm happy," she said lamely.

"It's so nice to be with someone who's not constantly competing with me," Sammy said, giving Alana another quick kiss on the lips. "You always take pride in my successes. That's why I like being around you."

Alana slumped slightly in her chair and took a bite of the slice of pizza Zach had thrown onto her plate. It was best to keep food in her mouth so she couldn't talk. After all, there really was no response to something like that.

Just then Stella prodded Alana in the ribs and looked over toward the door. "Is that Connor?" she whispered in Alana's ear.

Alana glanced up, and immediately her eyes linked with his. It was him all right, ambling right for them with his thick hair swaying slightly and his eyes twinkling.

"Oh my God," Stella whispered under her breath. "You weren't kidding. Look at him. He's incredible."

Alana was already looking at him. Stella was right. Connor hadn't made any obvious effort to dress for the evening, and yet, in his pale blue, ripped jeans and plain, white T-shirt, he looked as though he'd walked right out of a magazine.

"If you think he looks good that way, you should see him without his shirt on," Alana whispered to Stella conspiratorially.

Sammy glared at her. "Excuse me?"

"Relax," Stella assured him. "She invited him here for *me*. He's a handyman at one of her clients' places. He works with his shirt off when it's hot."

"Oh, a *handyman*," Sammy repeated.

"What's that supposed to mean?" Alana asked Sammy.

Before Sammy could reply, Connor stepped up to the table and planted a small peck on Alana's cheek. Strange. He'd never done that before. Even stranger, she was sure she could feel his lips there long after he'd moved away.

"Hey, Alana," he greeted her.

"You made it," Alana replied with obvious enthusiasm.

"I told you I would," he said with a grin. Then grabbing a chair, he placed himself right between Stella and Alana. "You mind if I squeeze in here?" he asked.

"No, that's perfect," Alana assured him. She jiggled her chair a little closer to Sammy to make room. "Connor, this is Stella," she said, pointing to her best friend.

"Hi," Connor said, turning his head to face her. "It's great to finally meet you. Alana's told me a lot about you."

"Likewise," Stella responded.

"I hope she only told you the good things," Connor joked.

"You have no idea," Stella replied with a laugh.

Sammy reached over Alana to shake

Connor's hand. "Sam Arden," he introduced himself. "I'm sure Alana's told you all about me as well."

A smirk formed on Connor's lips. "Sam . . . Sam . . . ," he repeated as if trying to recollect any mention of him. "Uh, yeah. I think I've heard of you."

Alana poked Connor in the ribs. "Cut it out. You know I told you all about Sammy."

Connor laughed. "Yeah, you did. Columbia guy, right?"

Sammy nodded. "That's me. Funny, Alana never mentioned you to me, though."

"Connor and I just met this week," Alana explained. "And you and I didn't get to talk until today. So I didn't get a chance."

Sammy nodded. "That makes sense. I guess I'll have to find more time to talk to you if I want to keep up with your new life."

"*You're* the one with the new life," Alana reminded him. "I'm still running with the same old crowd."

"And Connor," Sammy pointed out. "And that guy Leo." He placed a strong arm around Alana's shoulders and pulled her close. She smiled contentedly. It was nice to know she could still make him jealous—

even when there was nothing for him to be jealous of.

"Leo?" Connor asked, his eyebrows rising slightly in a playful, curious way.

"A fellow dog walker. We hang out at the dog run in Riverside Park sometimes," Alana explained. She started to giggle.

"What's so funny?" Sammy asked her.

"Oh, just this conversation Leo and I heard at the dog run the other day," Alana explained. "This woman Margaret was so totally freaked-out because her dog was rejected from a school she applied to."

"A *dog* school?" Stella asked incredulously.

"Oh yes, a dog school," Alana told her. "And not just any dog school, mind you. This was Paws Prep School."

"Oh, come on, this is a joke, right?" Connor asked.

Alana shook her head. "I'm serious. It's an obedience-training school. Very hard to get into. And this woman had gotten a rejection note from them in the mail. She was devastated."

"Because an obedience school rejected her dog?" Connor sounded amazed.

Alana shook her head. "They didn't reject

her dog. They rejected her! The school said she and her husband didn't seem like the kind of family they liked to work with at Paws Prep. I'm telling you, this woman was crushed. She was actually crying. And Leo and I were . . . well, we couldn't help but start cracking up. I was able to sort of bury my head in my shirt, but Leo . . . I swear. I really thought he was going to pee in his pants, he was laughing so hard. I mean, do you believe these people?"

"Can you imagine what a school like that must cost?" Stella asked. She was laughing now too.

"I know," Alana agreed. "It's ridiculous. Someone should write a book about New York's wealthiest dog families."

"Forget it. No one would believe it!" Stella told her.

"I barely believe it, and I *know* people like that," Connor chimed in.

"I don't see what the big deal is," Sammy remarked flatly.

Alana, Connor, and Stella all stopped laughing at once.

"You're kidding, right?" Stella asked him.

"No," Sammy said. "These people didn't steal their money; they worked for it. And they have the right to spend it any way they want."

"But they can train their own dogs," Stella said. "Or take a class at the ASPCA. They don't need some fancy, private dog school."

"Private dog school," Alana repeated, choking on her laughter. "I can just see the beagles and bloodhounds in their uniforms."

"With blazers and ties," Connor added.

"Only for the boys," Alana reminded him. "The girls would have to wear skirts."

"I'm serious," Sammy insisted. "Who are you to criticize these people for wanting the best?"

"The money they spend could be used for so many more important things," Stella told him. "Like helping Greenpeace save the rain forest. Or helping Habitat for Humanity buy more materials to build houses for the homeless."

"I'm sure that woman at the dog run gives money to charity," Sammy said. "She can take charitable donations as a tax deduction."

"Gee, that sounds so magnanimous," Stella replied sarcastically. "The rich give money to charity so they don't have to pay taxes."

"I don't care why they give, as long as they do," Alana said, trying to help Sammy out of this awful argument. "At Helping House we don't question anyone's motives for giving. We just take their cash. No questions asked."

"Speaking of Helping House," Connor interrupted. "How was the carnival today?"

"What carnival?" Sammy asked.

"You know, the one they have every year at Helping House," Alana reminded him. "I asked you if you wanted to help, remember? But you had the game to go to this afternoon." She turned to Connor. "Last year Sammy helped out at the cotton-candy machine. He kept giving the kids from the shelter oversize helpings. They were sugar crazed all night long."

"I remember," Sammy replied. "That was a fun day."

"You make it sound like it was a hundred years ago," Stella groaned. "It was only last fall."

"How'd you know about that?" Sammy demanded of Connor, ignoring Stella's comment completely.

"Alana mentioned it the other day," Connor explained simply. "I guess it just stuck in my head. It sounds like a great organization. Too bad it's even necessary, though. What kind of a guy would abuse his family? Doesn't make any sense."

"A lot of things don't make sense," Sammy said dismissively. He turned to Alana. "Did Helping House make a lot of money today?" he asked her.

Alana nodded. "There are always loads of people at that benefit. Even more importantly, the kids from the shelter had a blast."

"I wish I could have been there to take some shots of their faces," Connor said. "But I had something else scheduled."

"Something break down?" Sammy asked him.

Connor looked at him strangely. "Break down . . . ?" he began curiously. Then he paused. "Oh, no. I was actually shooting some head shots for an actor in my building. I do that sometimes for people I know. Starving actors don't have a lot of cash."

"Connor's a photographer," Alana told Stella.

"Yeah, you mentioned that earlier," Stella replied. "A few times, actually."

"Here comes the meatball pie!" Zach shouted, interrupting.

"Oh, yum!" Stella said, diving in for a slice.

"There's this awesome pizza place up near Columbia," Sammy told them. "It's off on a side street, and you wouldn't know it was there unless someone told you, but they make the most incredible Sicilian pie."

"Mmm . . . I love Sicilian. We've got to go there one night," Alana suggested.

"Absolutely," Sammy replied. He turned his attention back to Connor. "I guess between working as a handyman and taking pictures, you don't go to college."

Connor shrugged. "It's not for me. High school was enough formal education, I guess. I'm not one for sitting behind a desk. But I take photography classes at the New School a couple of nights a week."

"That sounds like fun," Stella said.

"You know what you want to be, and you're going for it," Alana agreed.

"Just like me," Sammy interjected. "I'm actually here celebrating my new internship—in the marketing department at Shoreman

Sporting Goods," he boasted to Connor. "It was pretty competitive, but I pulled it off. I think I even beat out a few upperclassmen."

Alana forced a smile to her lips. She was having a hard time with the whole Shoreman thing, but she felt she had to support Sammy. It was his life and his choice, and if it made him happy, then it should make her happy, too. Unfortunately, it wasn't working that way.

"This internship actually doesn't pay, but the next one I get will," Sammy explained. He ran his fingers through Alana's hair. "And then we'll be able to go to places that serve more than pizza."

"I *like* pizza," Alana assured him.

"Me too," Connor agreed, reaching over and taking a slice of the meatball pie. "That's something pretty much everyone has in common."

Sammy agreed and grabbed a slice of his own, which he scarfed down pretty quickly. A few minutes later he stood up. "I gotta make a quick call. The reception's lousy in here, though," he said. "Be back in a second."

"Okay," Alana said, wiping a bit of pizza grease off her chin and taking a sip of her

Diet Coke. As he walked away, she turned her attention back to her matchmaking scheme. "Stella, tell Connor all about the recycling project you're heading at school. It's so cool. I swear, Stella's going to save this whole planet single-handedly."

"No one can save it single-handedly," Stella corrected her. "We all have to work together. That's the whole point."

Alana listened for a few moments as Stella explained about their drive to force the school to stop using Styrofoam cups and to provide recycling bins for scrap paper, but her mind drifted. After a few minutes she realized Sammy had been gone awhile, and she hoped nothing was wrong.

"I'll be right back," she told Stella and Connor; then she got up and headed toward the door, to see if he was okay.

Seven

As she neared the entrance of the restaurant, Alana could hear Sammy talking on the phone. Obviously, his conversation was going on longer than he'd expected. No big deal. She turned to go back to her seat but stopped when she overheard what he was saying.

"Just give me a few more minutes, Tamara," he pleaded into the phone. "It's my old, high school friends. No. It's not like it's a big deal to me. But it is to them. They look up to me. I'm like a hero."

Alana could feel her blood start to boil. Old, high school friends? Like a hero? What the hell was he talking about?

"Okay, I'll be there in less than an hour,"

he said, obviously finishing up his conversation. Quickly Alana turned and hurried back to the table, not wanting to be caught eavesdropping.

"Whoa, you okay?" Stella asked as Alana flopped into her chair.

"Of course," Alana replied, trying to sound as normal as possible. "Why wouldn't I be?"

"I don't know," Stella said. "It's just that you don't normally dive-bomb into your seat like that."

Alana shook her head. "Don't be ridiculous."

"Hey, 'Lana, where's Sammy?" Evan called from the other end of the table.

"He's making a phone call," Alana called back. She was surprised at the sound of her own voice. It sounded kind of choked, like something was caught in her throat. She hoped no one noticed.

But Connor had. "Are you sure you're okay?" Connor asked her gently. "You don't sound like you. And you're kind of flushed."

"No. I'm definitely fine," she assured him, trying to flash him a smile. Connor returned her smile with a curious look, making it clear he didn't believe her.

A moment later Sammy reappeared at the table. "Hey, sorry I disappeared for so long," he apologized to Alana. "I had to make plans with a friend of mine. He needs help with his economics project."

Alana eyed him suspiciously. *His* economics project? Since when was a guy named Tamara?

"Anyway, I've gotta go," Sammy continued, avoiding her eyes by staring at his pizza.

"So soon?" Alana asked. "You practically just got here."

"I know, 'Lana. But this is kind of important," Sammy insisted.

Alana stared at him with surprise. He was lying. She knew it. And the worst part was he was doing it with such ease. What had happened to him in those first few weeks of college, anyway?

"I understand. Helping people's what I'm all about," she said weakly.

"And that's what I adore about you," Sammy said. He leaned over and planted a kiss on her mouth. Alana tried to kiss him back, but it was hard. She was angry. *Furious*, actually. But she was also too confused to confront him. Especially here, in front of all these people. Besides, he'd probably lie his way out of anything she said anyway.

"Yo, Sammy, splitting so early?" Zach asked.

"Got things to do, places to be," Sammy said.

"Are you going to homecoming?" Jessica asked him. "It's in two weeks."

"I'm gonna try," Sammy assured her. "But stuff comes up, you know?"

And with that, he was gone, leaving Alana all alone in the pizza place. Well, not alone exactly. But she might as well have been. Everyone else was having a good time, scarfing down pizza, chatting, and laughing. Even Connor and Stella seemed to be lost in an intense conversation.

Which was good. After all, that was what she'd been hoping for, right? Of course it was. Connor and Stella. That was the plan. And to help them along, Alana decided to get out of the way. Quickly she got up and dragged her chair down to the other end of the table near Rebecca and Evan. With her at the other end of the long table, Stella and Connor would have no one to talk to but each other.

About an hour later, Stella and Alana were back on the subway, heading home to the Upper West Side. "So was I right? Isn't Connor absolutely perfect?" Alana prodded.

Stella shrugged. "He's a nice guy."

Alana was amazed. "A nice guy? That's it?"

"That's it."

"But he's so interesting," Alana insisted. "And creative. And you have to admit he's gorgeous."

"Sure," Stella agreed. "He's all that. But there just weren't any fireworks going off between us. And besides, I think he's already into somebody else."

Oh. Alana hadn't counted on that. And for some reason, the thought of Connor being interested in some unknown girl made her uncomfortable. "What makes you think that?"

"He was talking about her all night," Stella answered. "And every time he mentioned her name, his eyes lit up."

Alana sighed. Lucky girl, whoever she was. "What's her name?" she asked Stella, trying not to sound overly curious.

Stella smirked. "Alana."

"Me?" Alana asked, her voice scaling up

slightly. "Don't be ridiculous. We're just friends."

"Maybe," Stella mused. "But I got the sense he'd like it to be more. You should have heard him going on and on about how wonderful it was that you volunteered with those abused women and their kids. And how great you were with animals."

"He was just making conversation," Alana assured Stella. "I'm the only thing the two of you have in common. What else was he going to talk to you about?"

"Gee, I don't know," Stella replied sarcastically. "The weather? The pizza? Whether there's life in outer space? There are plenty of things to talk about, Alana. But what he wanted to talk about was *you*. Well, you and Sammy, actually."

"What do you mean me and Sammy?"

"He asked me how long you guys had been together and whether or not I thought Sammy was good for you."

Alana wanted to ask Stella exactly what she had told Connor, but she stopped herself. It was better not to know. In fact, it was better to stop talking about Connor all together.

Not that she felt like talking about

Sammy at the moment either. Alana knew better than to tell Stella about the phone conversation she'd overheard. She'd definitely jump all over that. And besides, it was probably all an innocent misunderstanding, anyway. Something she and Sammy would laugh about some day. At least, that's what she hoped. Because the alternative was just too awful to imagine.

Eight

I've been thinking about it, and maybe
you and I should start seeing other people.
I'm not advocating breaking up completely,
but we're both young, and we need to
experience life a little more before we
settle down with one person. You may
really hate me for this right now, but
in a while you'll see I was right. If we
don't date other people, how can we
be sure that we're in this for all the right
reasons and not just settling for what's
comfortable?

Alana sat there on her bed, staring at the
e-mail, unable to move. Unable to speak.
Unable to *think*.

But Stella was far from speechless. She was furious. "What an asshole!" she exclaimed as she stared at the screen of Alana's laptop. "An e-mail? You date the jerk for three years, and he breaks up with you in an e-mail? He's such a chicken. He couldn't face you, so he did this." She wrapped her arm around Alana's shoulders. "I'm glad I was home when you called. You shouldn't have to go through this alone."

Alana didn't answer. She just sat there as the hot, salty tears began burning her eyes and trickling down her cheeks.

"It's not even a good e-mail. 'I'm not advocating breaking up.' What kind of pretentious crap is that?" Stella continued, her blood obviously boiling. "And it's a lie. Of course he's advocating a breakup. He's probably got his eye on someone already."

Alana nodded slowly. "He does. Her name's Tamara. I think he's been dating her for a while, actually."

"You knew about it?" Stella asked. "Since when? You never mentioned any suspicions to me."

"I only figured it out last night," Alana explained. "But I'd heard her name before."

Stella flopped down on the bed. "He was

never good enough for you," Stella told her. "Pretentious snob."

Alana thought about that. She pictured Sammy and herself at the antiwar protest in Central Park last summer. And at the Save Darfur rally in Washington, D.C. They'd gotten up at four in the morning just to make the bus for that one. In fact, Sammy had been the one to call her—three times!—on her cell phone, making sure she was out of bed and on time for that protest.

"Sammy was great for me, once," Alana said slowly. "But he's not Sammy anymore."

"I know," Stella agreed. "He's *Sam*." She held out her hand and imitated the phony, deep voice Sammy had used when he'd introduced himself to Connor last night. "And he works for child abusers."

"That's a little extreme," Alana suggested.

"Is it?" Stella said. "Could you—of all people—honestly date someone who worked for *Shoreman*?"

Alana shook her head.

"And how could you ever trust him again? If what you're saying is true, this whole let's-see-other-people thing is a little too after the fact. Seems like Sammy—

excuse me, I mean *Sam*—gave up his conscience when he went to college."

"Columbia has such an active student body. They're always holding protests, against the war or in favor of equal rights. I figured when Sammy went there . . . ," Alana's voice trailed off.

"He just got caught up in a snobby crowd," Stella told Alana.

"I guess it could happen to anyone," Alana remarked.

Stella shook her head. "Not to anyone. Not to you. Not to me. We are who we are. No one can change us. And that's the difference between us and him. You don't need him, Alana. You deserve a guy who knows who he is and stays true to himself. Not some slimy chameleon like Sammy."

Alana was surprised by how quickly Connor popped into her mind. But that was ridiculous. She hardly knew him. And besides, she had no way of getting in touch with him. No address, no phone number. So unless she happened to bump into him at the Beresford, she might not ever see him again.

Nine

Connor wasn't at the Beresford on Monday afternoon when Alana went to pick up Nicolette. She tried not to be too disappointed at not seeing him, but that was impossible. Stella's words kept running through her head: *What he wanted to talk about was you.*

Unfortunately, the last image Connor had of Alana was with Sammy by her side. He didn't know that Alana had just been unceremoniously dumped by Sammy. Or that she really wasn't nearly as upset by that as she thought she would—*or should*—be. Maybe it was the fact that Sammy had changed so much that he was nearly unrecognizable, or maybe it was just that she didn't have to see him every day in the halls at school, but either way, Alana felt surprisingly relieved that it was over—and that she hadn't had to be the one to break it off.

"Hey, Alana, over here!"

The sound of Leo's voice shook Alana from her thoughts. She looked around and spotted him on a bench near the water fountain in the Riverside Park dog run. Catching her eye, he smiled brightly and waved. Alana waved back and unfastened Nicolette's leash to set her free. The poodle looked up at her and then took off, running joyously through the sand in the dog run.

"You look like *you're* in a good mood," Alana said as she sat down on the bench beside him.

"Totally," Leo replied. He pulled a thin newspaper from his pocket. "I got my first article printed in the school paper."

Alana took the copy of the *Washington Square News* from his hands. It took her a minute to find the article, but she did, at the bottom of the third page. "RECORD NUMBER OF STUDENTS GET EXPERIENCE FROM INTERNSHIPS" BY LEO GARVIN. Alana paused for a minute. "You know, we've been hanging out here for, like, three months, and

I never knew your last name before."

"Well, now that you know something about me, you have to tell me something about you," Leo said.

"Like what?"

"Um . . . what's your favorite junk food?"

"Chocolate-covered, frozen bananas," Alana said. "I had them at Disney World once, and I became obsessed. They're really hard to find, though."

"Okay, I'll strike that off my list," Leo told her.

"Your list of what?" Alana asked him.

Leo grinned and looked into her eyes. "My list of things I'd like to get to know about you."

Something in the way he said that made Alana slightly uncomfortable. She knew Leo didn't—*couldn't*—have meant that the way it had sounded. They were just friends. Dog-walking compatriots. He wasn't interested in her that way. She was just imagining things. It must be the whole breaking-up-with-Sammy thing. It was playing tricks with her head. She looked down at the paper again. "This is really exciting, Leo!" she exclaimed, changing the subject.

"I know," Leo agreed. "You wouldn't

believe what a rush it was to see my name in print in a real newspaper. I mean, I know it's just a dumb little article—it's not going to win me a Pulitzer or anything—but it's a start, you know?"

Alana smiled warmly. "I know. It's awesome."

"Maybe next time I'll write an article that gets a photo with it," Leo continued. "The newspaper has some amazing photographers. And when people see a picture next to an article, they're more likely to read it."

Photographers. Alana's heart sank a bit, as thoughts of Connor swirled in her head. She took a deep breath and focused on reading the rest of Leo's article.

"Hey, you know what?" Leo asked. "Modern Art—that band you came to hear the other night—is playing at the Red Rooster two weeks from Friday. Maybe you could come. I mean, you could bring that Sammy guy if you want."

Alana frowned. "I can come, but may I bring someone else?"

"Sure, I guess," Leo said. "Sammy busy?"

"I wouldn't know," Alana said flatly. "We broke up. Well, actually, he broke up with me."

"Oh, wow," Leo said. "I had no idea. I'm sorry. I never would've mentioned him if . . ."

"Don't worry about it," Alana said, giving Leo a gentle smile. "You had no way of knowing. And anyhow, it's cool. For the best, you know."

Leo nodded. "Oh, totally. You were too good for him anyway."

"How would you know that?" Alana wondered. "You only talked to him for a second."

Leo shrugged. "That's all it took. I think you need a guy who's a little more into you and less into himself. Someone a little more creative and interesting. Someone who's got more interests than just money and preppy clothes."

Alana looked at him strangely. The someone Leo was describing sounded a lot like Connor. But that would be impossible. Leo didn't know Connor. She'd never even mentioned him. Alana shook her head slightly. Man, she really had to get Connor off her mind. And fast. The last thing she needed right now was a rebound relationship. What a mess *that* would be. Besides, she didn't even know if Connor would want a relationship with her. They had known each other only a week. That was too soon for anyone with a brain in her head to even think about something like that.

"Yo. Earth to Alana," Leo called out, waving his hand in front of her face.

"What? Oh. Sorry. I was daydreaming," Alana said.

"Guess you got a lot on your mind," Leo remarked kindly.

Alana shrugged.

"Oh, I almost forgot," Leo said suddenly, reaching into the pocket of his jean jacket and pulling out a sky blue flyer. "Someone on campus gave me this. I was thinking of volunteering an hour or two a week, and I thought it would be fun if we could do it together."

Alana looked down at the paper. "'Operation Dog Adoption,'" she read.

"It's a no-kill shelter on the Lower East Side," Leo explained. "They need people to come and play with the dogs and walk them and stuff."

Alana thought about that. The folks at Helping House really didn't need her as much now that the big carnival was over. That was their major fund-raiser of the year. And now that she didn't have to leave her weekends free for Sammy, she did have some extra time on Saturdays and Sundays. Besides, it was probably better to keep busy than just wallow in self-pity.

"You don't have to work there a lot of hours. Maybe just a little while on a Sunday or something," Leo continued.

"Sure, why not?" Alana said.

"Really?" Leo sounded surprised—and thrilled.

Alana nodded. "You want me to meet you there on Sunday?"

"Yeah. Definitely. I was thinking of going over at one," Leo told her. "That'll give me time to study in the morning."

"Okay, I'll be there," Alana agreed. She turned her head slightly and caught sight of Muffy, a little Yorkshire terrier who was a regular at the Riverside Park run. "Oh, man, check out what Cecilia has Muffy wearing today," Alana said, pointing toward the spot where Muffy was cowering beneath a bench.

"I'd hide too if someone made me wear that thing," Leo agreed. "The other dogs are probably all making fun of her."

Alana knew just what he meant. For some unknown reason, Cecilia had dressed her poor little dog in a red coat with black polka dots all over it. Two small wings jutted out from the back of the coat. "I think she's supposed to be a ladybug," Alana suggested with a grimace.

A moment later Cecilia ran over to Muffy and scooped her up from under the bench. "You dropped your hat," she cooed as she placed a red cap with black antennae on the dog's head.

"Yep, she's a ladybug," Alana remarked. She began to laugh.

"Why in the world would anyone want to dress their dog in a costume like that?" Leo wondered.

"A lot of people do," Alana told him. "Have you seen that new store on Broadway? I think it's called The Posh Pup. It's all dog clothes and costumes. And get this—they even have a dry-cleaning service."

"For *dog* clothes?" Leo sounded incredulous.

"Uh-huh," Alana informed him. "I didn't believe it either when I saw it. But I read all about it when I was at the store picking up Noodles's pumpkin costume. Mrs. Parker is going to make him wear it on Halloween."

"A bulldog dressed as a pumpkin," Leo mused. "I'm trying to picture it."

"Don't bother," Alana remarked, rolling her eyes. "It's too upsetting. I promised Noodles I'd take him to a different dog run on Halloween—so none of his friends will see him in it."

"Oh, I'm sure that made him feel much better," Leo teased.

Alana giggled. "I do what I can."

Leo glanced down at his watch. "I have to run," he told her suddenly. "Gotta get Pepper back home for dinner."

"Okay," Alana said. "You gonna be here on Wednesday?"

Leo nodded. "Definitely. With Princess and possibly Morpheus."

"Good," Alana replied. "It's not the same around here without you."

Leo grinned. "I feel the exact same way."

Alana could feel her heart beating faster as she approached the Beresford on Wednesday afternoon. Wednesday was usually a tough day—all four dogs at once. But it was also a day when she could pick up Nicolette, which meant there was the possibility that she might bump into Connor. Not that he'd been on her mind all day or anything. Just when she got up in the morning, and during gym class. And that time she'd found herself scribbling his name on her math notebook. But other than that, she hadn't thought of him once.

So why was it such a disappointment when she opened the door and there was no one in the Stanhopes' apartment but Nicolette? Maybe because wet kisses from a French poodle with bad breath weren't exactly what she'd been dreaming of the past few nights.

But it was all she was getting. That was for sure. And Alana figured she should be grateful for the affection. After all, the dogs were pretty much the only ones loving her these days. Not that she'd expected Connor to instantly fall in love with her like some fairy-tale prince or anything. Just a date would be nice. But since he didn't have her number and all she knew about him was that he worked in one of the hugest apartment buildings on the Upper West Side and lived somewhere in the East Village, that didn't seem too likely. Especially since she'd made such a big deal about having a boyfriend and trying to fix him up and all. Oh, man, she could kick herself for that. If only she had known that Sammy was about to set her free.

Alana stopped for a minute and thought about that. What a strange way to put it. Set her free. Almost as though she'd felt trapped by Sammy. But she hadn't. Had she? Well, maybe a little bit, toward the end, anyhow. Alana sighed as she locked the gate to the dog run before unleashing Curly, Noodles, Nicolette, and Frisky. It didn't matter now anyway. Twenty-twenty hindsight wasn't going to change anything. And to make matters worse, Leo wasn't even at the dog run. Alana would have to hang out with the owners. She was definitely not in the mood to hear them complaining about how there were no beef biscuits left at the Barkery that day or some other nonsense. Not when she had real problems.

"Okay, snap out of it," Alana scolded herself. After all, she knew better than most people what a real problem was. And the lack of a boyfriend didn't even come close to what the kids at Helping House faced. Besides, life was full of surprises. A new boyfriend could be waiting just around the corner.

"Hey, Alana!"

She jumped as a man's voice echoed across the busy dog run. For a minute her heart jumped. Could it be? . . .

No. It was just Leo. Not that she wasn't glad to see him. A good friend was exactly the medicine Alana needed right now to knock this self-pity right out of her. "Hi, Leo," she greeted him. Then she glanced at his chest and started laughing. "Nice sweatshirt," she added, appreciating the design on the front, which read DOG CRAP HAPPENS.

Leo grinned proudly. "I thought it was appropriate."

"So, how come you're so late today?" Alana asked. "You're usually here way before I am."

Leo reached into his knapsack and pulled out a long white bag with a silver foil lining. "I was picking this up," he said, handing it to her.

Alana opened the bag and pulled out a frozen, chocolate-covered banana. "Oh, wow! Where'd you get this?"

"There's a place over on Seventy-second Street that has them. It's probably not as good as the one you had in Disney World, but . . ."

Alana took a bite of the chocolate-banana concoction. "It's scrumptious!" she exclaimed. She reached over and hugged him tightly.

"Well, that made it all worth it," Leo said with a grin.

"You want a bite?" Alana asked him.

Leo shook his head. "What kind of gentleman would I be if I took a bite of my own gift? It's all yours."

"Oh, you have no idea how badly I needed this today," Alana said, taking another bite.

"Why? Bad day?"

"The worst," Alana assured him. For a moment she considered telling him about Connor, but she thought better of it. *Why bring it all up again?* "But it's all good now," she told Leo, taking another bite of her frozen banana.

"Glad I could help," Leo told her. He looked out into the yard. "Curly's looking spiffy today," he remarked, glancing over at the cocker spaniel.

"She spent her morning at Canine

Canyon," Alana said. "She got the full works, bubble bath, haircut, pedicure, and massage."

"And you brought her to the dog run?" Leo asked, kicking at the dirty sand beneath his feet.

"I figured she wanted to show off her new look," Alana replied playfully. She pointed toward where Curly was parading around with her nose in the air, as though she knew she looked really fine today. "See? Besides, a girl never knows when the right guy will suddenly appear."

"Is that why you're wearing that sweater?" Leo asked her. "Just in case?"

Alana blushed, surprised that Leo had noticed what she was wearing. Guys usually didn't catch stuff like that. But then again, Leo wasn't really like a guy-guy. He was more like just a good friend. Sort of like a Stella at the dog park.

Truth be told, she *was* actually wearing a new pink sweater. Usually she wore old, crappy clothes to walk the dogs, but she'd put the sweater on at the last moment—just in case. But she could have been wearing a ratty, old sweatshirt and ripped jeans for all it mattered today. Connor wasn't there.

"Nah," she told Leo. "I'm not expecting anyone to pop out of the bushes." *Not anymore, anyway,* she thought disappointedly.

Ten

ALANA

Alana was surprised to see the note on the bulletin board in the Stanhopes' kitchen when she returned Nicolette later that afternoon. It was very unusual for either Mr. or Mrs. Stanhope to have come home at any point in the day, but one of them must have, because the note hadn't been there before. Mr. Stanhope was probably the one to have left the note because the handwriting wasn't the familiar tiny print Mrs. Stanhope used on her notes. This was bolder, darker handwriting. She pulled the note from the board and unfolded the paper.

Sorry I missed you. Tried to
get to the apartment b4
you picked up Nic, but I
got held up. Give me a call.
—C

Alana stood there for a minute, cheeks
flushed, feet glued to the floor, staring at
the phone number he'd scribbled at the bottom of the note. Connor had come looking
for her. He'd made it his business to let
himself into the Stanhopes' apartment and
leave her a note. He was probably taking a
big chance. Suppose she hadn't seen the
note? Suppose Mr. or Mrs. Stanhope had
gotten to it first? They probably wouldn't
have liked the fact that one of the building's
workers had let himself into their apartment for no apparent reason. But he'd
risked it. For her! Which made this little
note so incredibly sweet.

Arf! Arf! Nicolette's barking got Alana's
attention. "Oh, you poor thing. You must be
starving," Alana said, opening the refrigerator door and pulling out a container of beef-
barley stew. She emptied it into the dog's
dish, filled the water bowl with cold Evian,

and walked toward the door. Nicolette padded closely behind, with a red rubber Kong toy in her mouth.

"Sorry, Nic, no can do," Alana told the poodle. "I gotta run. I have a very important call to make."

A half hour later Alana was sitting on her bed with her cell phone in her hand, staring at the note Connor had left. Somehow, she was having the hardest time dialing the number. She didn't know why, exactly. It wasn't like she'd never called a guy before. She used to call Sammy all the time, no prob. But for some reason this was different.

But why? She had no idea what Connor wanted. For all she knew, he just wanted to ask her about doing some photography at the Helping House shelter or something. No big deal. She picked up the phone and began to press the numbers. 1-646 . . .

Then again, if that was all he wanted, she'd be devastated. She clicked the red off button on her cell phone . . . for about the nineteenth time.

"Okay, this is ridiculous," Alana told herself. "What are you, in seventh grade?

You're almost a college student. Grow up and dial the number." Alana rolled her eyes. "Great. Now I'm talking to myself. This guy's making me crazy." She held her breath and began to dial once again. 1-646 . . .

The phone rang once and then went directly to voice mail. "Hi. Connor here. I'm so bummed I missed your call. Leave your name and number, and I'll call you back."

Alana took a deep breath as she waited for the *beep.* . . . "Connor, it's Alana. I got your note, and I'm . . . um . . . calling you. Call me back." Her voice shook as she left him her phone number.

As she hung up the phone, Alana fell back on her bed and covered her face with her pillow in embarrassment. *Okay, so that was the dumbest message ever left by anyone ever in the history of the telephone. Of course I got his note. How else would I have gotten his number? And why did I bother giving him my number? He'd have it on his missed-call list on his cell. He's going to think I'm a moron. He's never gonna call me back. I wouldn't even call me back after that. . . .*

"At the end of the world, you're the last thing I see. . . ." Alana jumped at the sound of her

ring tone. Her heart began pounding as she picked up her phone and glanced at the screen. Stella.

Oh. Well, of course it wasn't him, she thought. *His phone wasn't even on. It had been only two seconds since she'd called and left a message on his phone.*

She clicked the green talk button. "Hey, Stel."

"Gee, could you sound any less excited to hear from me?" Stella joked.

"Sorry. I was expecting . . ." Alana let her voice trail off. She wasn't actually expecting anyone.

"Expecting who?" Stella asked.

"It's nothing. Just that Connor left me a note with his phone number, so I called him. But he wasn't home," Alana explained feebly.

"You mean Connor who you're not at all interested in?" Stella teased. *"That* Connor?"

"Well, I didn't say I wasn't interested in him. I . . ."

"That's exactly what you said," Stella reminded her. "But it's okay. You were in denial, because of the *evil one.*"

"Sammy's not evil," Alana replied.

"Why are you defending him?" Stella

asked.

Alana didn't answer. She didn't *have* an answer, actually. His behavior lately was kind of indefensible.

"So the hottie left you his digits," Stella said, changing the discussion back to the topic at hand. "Cool."

"I guess," Alana said. "I don't know what he wants, though."

"He wants *you*," Stella said. "God, sometimes you are *so* thick."

"Well, it doesn't matter, because I'm not ready to get into anything with anyone right now," Alana insisted. "It's too soon."

"So, take it slow," Stella said. "Don't stick your tongue down his throat until *after* dinner."

"Ha ha. Very funny," Alana groaned. "I don't even know if I like him that way. . . ."

"Sure," Stella said doubtfully. "I could see why you wouldn't. He's just awful. Who would want a gorgeous guy who's funny, talented, and hardworking? A guy who remembers what you're doing on the weekends, when you just mention it once."

Alana sighed. It *was* kind of nice the way he'd remembered about her being at the carnival last Saturday.

"And I don't know why you'd ever want a guy who is willing to work hard for what he wants, instead of a jerk like Sammy who'll probably wind up stuck in a cubicle crunching numbers for a huge conglomerate that swallows up small companies for sport," Stella continued.

"Well, Connor definitely works hard," Alana said, recalling how sweaty he'd been when he'd been fixing the curtain rod at the Stanhopes' the day she'd met him. His skin was all tan and shiny with perspiration. . . . *God.* Just the thought of it was a turn-on.

Just then there was a beeping on the other end. "Oh no. That's my call-waiting. What if it's him?"

"Him? You mean *Connor*? The guy you're not even sure you like?" Stella joked.

"Shut up," Alana squawked. She pulled the phone away from her ear to check the name on the phone screen. "Oh, God. It *is* him. What do I do?"

"Try answering it," Stella suggested.

"But what do I say?"

Stella laughed. "Start with hello. As for me, I'm saying good-bye." And with that she hung up, leaving Alana on her own.

She took a deep breath and clicked the green talk button. "Hello . . . ," she said quietly.

"Alana?" Connor asked.

"Yeah. Hi, Connor." Alana was barely getting the words out.

"Oh. You didn't sound like you for a minute."

Of course not. I'm freaking out, she thought. But out loud she said, "It's definitely me."

"Good." Connor chuckled. "Because that's exactly who I felt like talking to."

"Same here," Alana said, sounding much more enthusiastic than she'd expected.

"I just wanted to tell you I had a great time with your friends last weekend," Connor said.

"They liked you, too," Alana said.

"Well, most of them did, anyway," Connor corrected her. "I didn't get the feeling Sam was too fond of me."

"That's okay," Alana told him flatly. "*I'm* not too fond of *him* these days."

"Why? What happened?" Connor asked.

"Well—we—he—," Alana stammered nervously. She didn't exactly want to tell Connor that she'd been unceremoniously dumped in an e-mail and that she hadn't heard from Sammy since. "Let's just say he and I were going in separate directions, and we decided to end things."

"Oh, wow. I'm sorry," Connor told her.

"You are?" Alana asked, surprised.

Connor chuckled. "Not really. I mean, I feel bad if you're sad, but honestly Alana, the guy's a jerk."

"He wasn't always," Alana murmured feebly. She was getting tired of defending him to everyone.

"I'm sure," Connor replied. "You wouldn't have been with him so long if he'd always been like that."

Alana smiled. Finally someone was giving her credit for not being a total idiot for the past three years. "Yeah. Well, it's ancient history, anyway."

"I was never very good at ancient history," Connor told her. "But current events, man, I'm a whiz at that."

Alana laughed. "And what are you *currently* doing?" she asked him.

"At the moment, I'm getting up the guts to ask you out for Friday night," Connor replied honestly.

"Oh."

"I mean, if you're not doing anything,

that is. I know it's kind of short notice. My sister always told me girls liked to be called more than two days in advance, but I . . . well . . . I didn't find out about you and Sammy until just this second and . . ."

Alana smiled as she listened to his voice trail off. He sounded so nervous. Not at all as sure of himself as he'd seemed before. It really was kind of cute. She waited a beat and then finally put him out of his misery. "Actually, I happen to be free on Friday night."

"Really?" Connor asked. "That's awesome. What do you want to do? I mean, we could go to dinner and a movie, or . . ."

Alana sighed. Dinner and a movie. That could cost him a lot—especially since movies in New York were up to $11.50 a ticket now. Someone like Connor probably couldn't really afford to spend all that in one night.

"How about we do something really New York?" she suggested.

"Like what?"

"I was thinking we could take a ride on the Staten Island Ferry."

"You're serious?" Connor asked her.

"Sure. It's so much fun, especially if it's

a nice night," she assured him. *And it's free,* she thought. But, of course, she would never say that. It might hurt his pride. Guys could be kind of weird about things like money.

"Oh," Connor said slowly. "You've done that before." He sounded kind of bummed.

"No," Alana said quickly. "I mean, not on a date. I've been on it with a bunch of friends a couple of times."

"I've actually never been on the ferry," Connor admitted.

"Well, after Friday night you won't be able to say that anymore," Alana told him. "It'll be fun. A whole new experience."

"That's exactly what I was hoping for," Connor agreed. "Something new and exciting."

Alana raced up the subway stairs at top speed, hoping Connor would still be there. They'd planned to meet at eight o'clock at the Whitehall station, which was right near the ferry. But it was already 8:10. Connor may have figured she wasn't coming or something. And since she'd been underground, her cell phone hadn't had reception so he could reach her.

Not that the lateness was completely her fault. Okay, sure she'd changed her shirt at least six times before finally settling on the soft, creamy beige, cashmere, short-sleeved sweater, tight jeans, and cowboy boots. But she still could have made it on time if the stupid train hadn't stayed at the Thirty-fourth Street station for what seemed an eternity.

"Alana, over here!"

Connor's deep voice rang out through the air as Alana emerged from the subway into the dark New York night. She looked in the direction of the sound and spotted him leaning against a streetlamp. The light above provided a glow around him, as though he were one of the angels in those gilded paintings in the Metropolitan Museum. Alana thought he was quite possibly the most magnificent thing she'd ever seen.

"I'm so sorry I'm late," she apologized, gasping for air as she came rushing over toward him.

"It's okay. It was worth the wait. You look gorgeous." He took her by the hand. "Come on. Let's get on the boat."

Alana was glad it was night. Otherwise, he might have seen how fiercely she was blushing. As it was, she hoped he couldn't hear her heart pounding or feel the sudden tingling that was going through her fingers as her hand touched his.

When they turned the corner and the big orange boat came into view, Connor reached into his pocket with his free hand and pulled out his wallet.

"What are you doing?" Alana asked him.

"I'm gonna buy tickets," Connor explained.

"There are no tickets," Alana said. "The Staten Island Ferry is free."

"Free?" Connor asked. "You're kidding."

Alana shook her head. "Nope. Totally free. I can't believe you didn't know that."

Now it was Connor's turn to blush. "Guess you learn something new every day."

"Oh, I didn't mean that the way it sounded," Alana said. "I just meant, well, you know . . . ," her voice trailed off.

"I don't mind learning things from you," Connor assured Alana. He threw her a cocky grin and pulled her a little closer. "You never know, someday there may be one or two things I can teach you, too."

"I'll bet there are," Alana agreed, enjoying tremendously the feeling of his hip touching hers.

They boarded the ferry, and Alana led Connor to the highest deck. "You get the best views from here," she told him, moving toward the back of the boat as it pulled away from the dock.

Connor looked directly into her eyes. "I already have the best view," he told her sincerely.

Alana blushed, again. She couldn't remember blushing this much in her whole life. "Wait until you see the Statue of Liberty all lit up," she said.

"Aah, who needs a big, green, metal woman, when I've got a gorgeous, flesh-and-blood one right here," Connor said. He ran his finger gently across her cheek, leaving a trail of tingles in its path.

Alana felt as though she could barely breathe. She glanced up into the night sky. The air above the harbor was clear and crisp. "What an amazing half-moon."

"Mmhmm," Connor said, moving even closer toward her. "It's a magnificent night."

Alana took a deep breath, inhaling the faint scent of his aftershave. It was kind of spicy, with a touch of lemon or orange. She knew that from now on, that smell would always remind her of him. Of this night. Of their first kiss . . .

Alana knew he was going to kiss her even before his lips touched hers. It was something in his eyes, the way they were peering into hers, searching for her silent permission. Alana looked back into his eyes, hoping she was giving him the signal he needed.

A moment later his lips were on hers. He kissed her gently at first, a series of small, curious pecks, really. And then, when he was sure she wanted the same thing he did, he kissed her harder, pulling her close, tangling his hands in her long, flowing, golden brown hair. Alana clung tightly to him as they kissed, enjoying the feel of his strong arms around her. She wished they could stay like this forever, never having to let go.

The sudden banging of the ferry as it pulled into the Staten Island terminal shocked Alana back into reality. Had they made the trip across the harbor already? Was that possible?

"Mmm," she moaned quietly as she

pulled away from him. "We're, um, here."

Connor looked up at the bright terminal light. "Where?" he asked.

"In Staten Island," Alana told him. "We have to get off."

Connor shook his head. "Let's just stay on. Ride back to Manhattan." His voice sounded quiet and hoarse.

Alana knew what he meant. She never wanted to get off this boat. She just wanted to ride back and forth forever, safely encased in Connor's arms. "We can't," she said quietly. "We have to get off and reboard. That's the rules."

"I hate rules," Connor said with a sigh. "Always have."

"We can get right back on," Alana assured him. But she knew the mood had been broken. They would never be able to get that feeling back. The first kiss can never be completely repeated.

Still, as Alana discovered on the trip back to Manhattan, a second kiss can be pretty amazing too.

Connor insisted on bringing Alana back to the Upper West Side, even though she'd insisted that she could take the subway all by herself. In fact, he'd wanted to take her home in a taxi, but she'd insisted on the train. Ever since the fare hike, cabs were outrageously expensive, and besides, the express train could have them uptown in just a few minutes.

Seventy-second Street was crowded and bustling when Connor and Alana emerged from the train station. People were milling all around, heading into restaurants or over to the multiplex on Sixty-eighth Street for the late show.

"You hungry?" Connor asked Alana.

"Mmmhmm. Starved," Alana replied. "Must be being on the water or something."

"Where do you feel like going?"

"There's Gray's Papaya," Alana said, pointing to the huge, yellow hot-dog stand that covered most of the corner at Seventy-second and Amsterdam. "They have the best hot dogs in the city."

Connor looked at her curiously. "All you want is a hot dog?"

Alana nodded. "With mustard and relish."

"What, no onions?" Connor asked.

"No," Alana said. "I don't want—" She blushed prettily, her tongue getting all tangled in her words.

Connor laughed. "I appreciate the restraint on the onions," he told her. "I won't have any either."

Since there were no tables at Gray's Papaya and no place to stand by the counter, Alana and Connor grabbed their franks and drinks and ran across the street to the small park. They sat down on a bench beneath a streetlamp and watched as the people walked by. For some reason, there seemed to be aging hippies everywhere. Middle-aged men with bald heads and long, gray ponytails were walking side by side with women in long, Indian-print skirts.

"The Allman Brothers must be at the Beacon Theater again," Alana deduced, pointing to the small rock venue down the block.

"The Allman Brothers are *always* at the Beacon," Connor joked. "Either them or some other really old band."

"It seems that way, anyway," Alana agreed. "My parents went to see the Allmans last month."

"Your parents are into the Allman Brothers?" Connor asked, sounding surprised.

Alana nodded. "And the Dead. Big

time. When I was a kid, we had so many pictures of Jerry Garcia around the house, I thought he was a relative."

Connor laughed. "So, you're the product of two hippie freaks."

"Pretty much," Alana admitted. "Except now they're lawyers, both with Legal Aid."

"Helping the poor fight the system," Connor noted with a grin. "Cool. I guess the apple doesn't fall far from the tree."

"Nope. We're all hopeless do-gooders in my family," Alana replied. "It's all about giving back. How about your folks?"

"Well, they're not into the Dead, I'll tell you that," Connor said. "They're not particularly into helping others, either. You probably wouldn't like them very much when you first met them. But once you got to know them . . . you'd totally dislike them."

Wow. That was pretty harsh. Obviously Connor had some issues with his parents. Alana decided to let the subject drop. They sat for a moment, quietly, until the silence became almost deafening.

"So, how's the college thing going?" Connor asked her finally.

Alana shrugged. "I'm doing applications. So far, I've finished the ones for NYU,

Hunter, and Columbia."

"They're all in New York," Connor noted.

"Yeah. I want to stay in the city. I figure I can save money by living at home for at least the first year. Then I can maybe get a place with a few roommates or move into a dorm."

"Oh, that's great!" Connor said. He paused awkwardly. "I mean, it's good that you're staying in the city."

Alana smiled. He was hoping she'd be in the city for a while. That was a very good sign.

Connor looked out into the bustling crowd. "I wish I had my camera," he said. "I could get some really cool shots—especially if I used a slow shutter speed. That guy underneath the red stoplight—the one in the bright, orange and yellow shirt and the green pants—kind of looks like someone Gauguin would paint if he were living in New York in 2008."

Alana looked at the guy beneath the light. She hadn't even noticed him. Even if she had, she certainly never would've thought of him in terms of a painting. To her he was just a weirdly dressed guy waiting for the light to change. There were probably a million anonymous people like him all over New York tonight. Well, anonymous to everyone but Connor, anyway.

"Do you see art in everything?" she asked incredulously.

Connor shrugged. "I guess. The thing about art is, it doesn't always have to be traditionally attractive to be beautiful, you know? Sometimes there can be an inner beauty, something that's really intense and speaks to people. Something they'd see too, if they would just take the time to look. I figure it's my job to *make* them look."

Alana stared at him for a moment, totally blown away. She'd never known anyone like Connor before. There was a certain irony in a guy who was so gorgeous on the outside spending his life looking for obscure *inner* beauty. But more amazing was the fact that Connor wasn't embarrassed talking about it. Most of the guys Alana knew would never open up about things like art and beauty—if they even thought about them. And she doubted they did.

Alana sat back and snuggled against his arm, feeling incredibly lucky to be there. He curved his hand over her shoulder and rested his head on hers. They grew quiet again, sitting close together on the park bench, looking at the old hippies and enjoying the pulse of the city. After a few minutes, though, Connor began to fidget slightly with his fingers.

"So . . . um . . . you maybe want to do this again sometime?" he asked, suddenly sounding shy and slightly apprehensive. *Very out of character.*

"What? Eat hot dogs on a bench in the middle of Seventy-second Street?" Alana teased.

"Very funny," Connor replied. "Didn't anyone ever tell you it's not nice to kid around with a guy when he's nervous?"

"Nervous about what?"

"Well, I had the most amazing time tonight," Connor said. "You're absolutely incredible. And I was kind of hoping you sort of felt the same way about me."

Was he kidding? She'd sort of made that pretty clear on the boat, hadn't she? Still, it was rather endearing to see him squirm a little. He was usually so sure of himself.

"Oh, yeah, I had a great time. And I think *you're* pretty incredible too," Alana assured him.

"So, you'd want to go out and do something again, then?" Connor asked.

"Sure."

Connor's whole body seemed to relax. "Cool. Um, you probably have plans for tomorrow, right?"

Alana nodded. "Yeah. I'm kind of busy."

"Well, we could do something next weekend," Connor said. "If you're free, that is."

"Next weekend?" Alana asked.

Connor tensed up again. "You're busy, right?"

Alana shook her head. "No. I was just hoping maybe I could see you sooner."

A big smile flashed across Connor's face. "Oh. Well, yeah. I could walk the dogs with you on Monday. I could meet you at the apartment and then . . ."

"You mean at the Stanhopes' apartment, right?" Alana asked.

"Yeah. Their place. And then we could take a walk in the Ramble," Connor suggested. "Sit in the woods, maybe?"

"Sure," Alana said. "I should be safe. I'll have Nicolette for a chaperone."

"You want a chaperone?" Connor wondered.

"Not really," Alana admitted. And to prove it, she leaned over and kissed away the bit of mustard he had on the corner of his mouth.

Eleven

Alana was still glowing the next morning as she took the train down to the dog adoption center where she was supposed to meet Leo. Every time she even thought about Connor, a flush rose to her cheeks and a smile formed on her lips. She was sure the people on the subway must have thought she was insane. But what the hell. This was New York. Everyone there was a little insane. It was part of the charm.

Leo was waiting for her outside the Operation Dog Adoption shelter. His face broke into a big smile as she approached the large, gray building. "Hey, you made it," he greeted Alana.

"Yep. Wouldn't miss it," she said. "I'm not late or anything, am I?"

Leo shook his head. "I actually got here early to sign us in." He held out a green cord with a white card attached to it and slipped it around her neck. "This is your ID. You have to wear it whenever you take a dog out of the shelter for a walk."

"So they know we're not just walking off with a pup, right?" Alana asked.

"Exactly. They're really careful about who takes the dogs in and out," Leo explained.

"This is a tough adoption process. They ask about a million questions on their adoption forms. And I heard them call references for one couple."

Alana nodded. "What kinds of dogs do they have in here?" she asked as she followed Leo inside and up to the front desk.

"It looks like mostly mixed breeds," he told her. "They're so sweet. I went in to feed a group of terrier-mix puppies, and they were jumping all over me. It was just supermarket dog food, but they were so incredibly grateful."

Alana thought of the way her clients pampered their dogs with fine cuts of beef and hand-prepared dog stews. She wondered if the spoiled Upper West Side dogs could ever be as grateful for anything as these dogs were for Alpo. "They say rescued dogs are always the sweetest to their owners because they never really forget what it's like to be abandoned," she told Leo.

"I know," he said. "I think I figured out what the hardest part of this job is going to be."

"Cleaning the cages?" Alana asked.

Leo shook his head. "The hardest part is going to be leaving without taking a few of these guys home with me. I'm telling you,

Alana, I've fallen in love at least three times this morning. Wait until you see this adorable cocker-beagle mix in the next room. She's just the most beautiful dog."

Leo wasn't kidding. The dog had a brown and white, spotted beagle body, except her ears were all curly and furry like a cocker spaniel's. Her face was pretty much cocker spaniel too, except her snout was longer. Alana bent down and put out her hand. The dog padded right up to her and snuggled against her thigh.

"They're calling her Delancey because she was found digging through the garbage near Delancey Street," Leo said.

"Oh, wow. I'm totally crazy about her," Alana said, scratching Delancey under the chin.

"Tell me about it," Leo agreed, looking intensely into Alana's blue eyes. Then he added quickly, "Lucky for you, Delancey's on our list for yard duty."

"What's yard duty?"

"It's kind of like taking them to a dog run," Leo explained, "except this yard is just for the shelter dogs. It's to get them acclimated to being around other dogs and with people. Most of these dogs have been all by themselves for a long time. They can't just be turned over to a family until the shelter thinks they're really domesticated."

"Delancey seems pretty mellow to me," Alana told him.

"Don't be fooled. You never know what will make a stray turn all of a sudden," Leo warned.

"You sound pretty knowledgeable about all this," Alana remarked, impressed.

"I came to a training meeting last night," Leo said. "I wanted to call you, but I realized I didn't have your cell number."

Alana blushed slightly, remembering the night before. "I was busy last night, anyway," she said.

"It's okay. I can fill you in on all the details once we get out in the yard. Come on, we've gotta go get the leashes."

"How far away is the dog run?" Alana asked him.

"It's just out back," Leo told her. "But we have to take the dogs for a walk on the street before they can go to the yard. That way they get used to being on a leash."

"So we're kind of trainers," Alana mused.

"Not exactly," Leo replied. "We're just

reinforcing what the trainers have been working on with the dogs."

"Wow. They've got their own trainers and their own yard. This place is some setup. I wonder if the dogs ever want to leave," Alana said.

"Sure they do," Leo assured her. "Everyone wants someone to belong to."

"Good girl, Delancey," Alana praised the beagle-cocker mix as she walked her down the block near the shelter. She waited patiently as Delancey sniffed every lamppost, mailbox, and hydrant before leaving her own scent in the mix. "It sure does take her a long time to sniff," she told Leo.

"Think of it like she's reading a chain letter," Leo explained, watching as his shepherd-mix dog lifted his leg to go. "All different dogs have left their scent. She just wants to know exactly who was there and then add her own to the chain."

"Wow, you learned a lot in that training class," Alana complimented him.

"Actually, I've done a lot of reading about dogs," Leo explained. "I figure if I'm going to walk them, I should probably understand them."

Now Alana was really impressed. She'd done very little reading on dogs, except for books on their safety. Basically, she worked on instinct. But it probably wouldn't hurt her to do some research like Leo had. It would make her a better dog walker. She made a silent vow to check a book or two about the psychology of dogs out of the library.

"Okay, I think they're finished with their walk," Leo said. "Why don't we take them back to the shelter and give them a little free time in the dog run?"

"Good idea," Alana agreed. "They're cooped up all the time in the shelter cages. They need a little freedom."

"Exactly," Leo said. "Let 'em be themselves for a while."

Alana followed Leo back into the shelter. They stopped at the desk and signed the dogs back. Then they followed the painted, orange paw prints on the floor back to the dog run behind the building.

There seemed to be a lot of volunteers and dogs in the small, chained-in yard behind the shelter. It wasn't the nicest dog run Alana had ever seen—just some sand and gravel with one tree in the middle. A few folding chairs had been spread around for the volunteers to sit in. And unlike the park run in Riverside Park, which had a view of the trees and grass (and the Hudson River if you looked past the West Side Highway bordering the park), this dog run had a view of the backsides of the neighboring restaurants and apartments. Still, for these dogs it was better than being caged up in the shelter all the time.

"Okay, Duke, you're free to run," Leo said, patting the shepherd mix on his long, sleek, gray-black back before removing his leash.

Alana gave Delancey a little kiss on the head. "You too, sweetie. Have some fun."

Delancey didn't have to be told twice. She ran off like a flash, eager to run with the other dogs.

Alana smiled. "Nice of you to say goodbye," she called after her jokingly. Then she and Leo pulled two chairs together and sat down.

"This is some place, huh?" Leo asked her.

"Yeah, really nice," Alana agreed. "I like that they try and train the dogs a little bit before giving them to people."

"It helps make sure the adoption will stick. They don't want people taking a dog home for a few days and then returning him."

Alana watched as Delancey jumped up and down, barking happily as she looked up toward the top of the tree. "I wish I could adopt her," she admitted.

"Do you have a dog of your own?" Leo wondered.

Alana shook her head. "Our apartment is kind of small, and my folks work a lot. With me going to college next year, well, eventually I'll move out, even if it's not right away. And then we'd have to hire a dog walker for the dog walker's dog. That doesn't seem right."

"I have a dog at my parents' house in Philly," Leo said. "Charlie. He's a springer spaniel. Best dog in the world. My younger sister's taking care of him while I'm at school."

"I didn't know you were from Phila-delphia," Alana told him. "I didn't know you had a younger sister, either."

Leo nodded. "Yeah. Her name's Sarah. She's in tenth grade now. Maybe you'll meet her sometime. She's supposed to come up and visit me this semester."

"I'd love to meet her," Alana told him.

"I think she'll probably stay in Philly for

school. She wants to go to Temple University. But I always wanted to live in New York. That's why I applied to NYU. And you know the rest of the story. Here I am."

"Yep," Alana replied. "Here you are! Is the city everything you hoped for?"

Leo looked at her and smiled deeply. "And more," he assured her in a deep, sincere voice. "Especially because . . ."

"DOG LOOSE!"

The sound of another volunteer's shout stopped Leo midsentence. He looked up and saw a brown and white dog chasing a squirrel on the other side of the fence. "It's Delancey," he said. "She dug her way underneath the fence. She must have seen a squirrel or something!"

"Oh no! Delancey! Delancey come back!" Alana shouted, running toward the fence.

"She doesn't know her name," a volunteer told Alana.

Alana blushed. Of course she didn't. She'd been at the shelter only a little while. Certainly not long enough to learn a name. Quickly Alana rushed toward the fence. "No! Stay!" she shouted at the dog. But Delancey had been on her own on the streets a long time. She wasn't great with commands from humans. The dog ignored Alana completely.

"I'll get her," Leo told Alana. He began climbing the chain-link fence. "Stay calm." In a moment he had dropped to the ground on the other side of the fence and was walking toward Delancey.

"What are you doing?" Alana shouted at him. "Don't walk, *run*. She's going to get away!"

"Running will scare her," Leo replied, in a voice as calm and relaxed as he could muster. He followed behind Delancey for a few feet, until the dog stopped and began sniffing a nearby fire hydrant.

That was when Leo made his move. He reached over and grabbed Delancey from behind. She struggled for a moment, letting out a few strong barks. But eventually she surrendered, laying her head helplessly on Leo's shoulder as he brought her back to the shelter.

It wasn't until Leo arrived back in the yard a few minutes later, after leaving Delancey inside with a shelter employee, that Alana realized she had barely been breathing. But the moment she saw Leo, she let out a huge sigh of relief. He was a hero. Without him,

Delancey could've been lost again, or worse.

Alana raced over and grabbed Leo. "Thank you, thank you," she whispered, hugging him tightly. Leo didn't say a word. He just wrapped his arms around Alana and kissed her. Alana kissed him back, relaying all the gratitude she had inside her. They stood there for a moment, in the middle of the dog run, their lips joined.

But Alana felt nothing. No tingle, no pounding heart. Just mouth on mouth. "Okay, that was weird," Leo said, jumping away from her.

From the disappointed look on Leo's face, Alana could tell he hadn't gotten much more out of the kiss than she had. "Gee, thanks," she said, trying to joke them both out of an extremely embarrassing situation.

"No, I just mean . . ."

"I know what you mean," Alana said kindly.

"I thought it would be different," Leo told her.

"You had actually thought about us kissing?" Alana asked incredulously.

Now it was Leo's turn to blush. "Yeah, I guess. Sometimes. Maybe. Didn't you?"

Alana kicked at the ground. Actually

Twelve

she never had. But saying that would just embarrass Leo even more. And frankly, she didn't think either of them could take any more discomfort. "Once in a while," she lied. "But at least now we know that we're better off being friends."

"We *are* still friends, right?" Leo asked her.

"Of course," Alana said. "Dog walkers united!"

Leo smiled. "Wow, who'd have thought the two of us would have absolutely no chemistry at all?"

Alana shrugged. "There's no explaining chemistry."

Certainly, there was no explaining Alana's chemistry with Connor. She'd barely known him two weeks, and already their relationship had advanced to the same level as her three-year relationship with Sammy. And not just physically—although she blushed just thinking about the way Connor's strong arms had felt around her waist and how the touch of his lips on hers had practically burned right through her. It was more the way they spoke to each other, laughing and joking as though they'd known each other for a hundred years.

They even had private jokes. "Now, you're sure you *bought* that bottle of water?" he had asked her teasingly during a walk through the Ramble with Nicolette on Monday afternoon. "You wouldn't want to get into the dog's stash or anything. The Stanhopes would flip if doggie dearest here had to drink from the tap!"

Alana giggled. "No, the water's mine. I only steal Nicolette's peanut butter– flavored bones," she assured him. "They're good for my teeth."

"Let me see," Connor said, pulling her close and examining her smile. "Yes, they're very white," he added before placing his mouth on hers and covering them completely.

"Arrffff!" Nicolette barked as she jumped up and down, trying to get between them as they kissed.

"I think she's jealous," Alana told him.

Connor pulled her closer and kissed her again, blatantly ignoring Nicolette's barking. "You have nothing to worry about," he assured Alana. "I'm completely smitten."

Smitten. *Mmm*. Alana loved the sound of that word. There was something so old-fashioned and elegant about it. As though she and Connor were some sort of lovers in a Jane Austen novel. The ones where the right people always wind up together in the end.

Nicolette pulled harder on the leash, and Alana acquiesced, allowing the dog to pull her farther into the Ramble. She watched as a bright orange leaf fell from a tree ahead and landed in the lake nearby. "God, it's gorgeous out here," she murmured, looking out at the rainbow of green-, orange-, yellow-, and red-leaved trees that surrounded the lake.

"Things look pretty gorgeous from this angle, too," Connor said. He was standing a few feet behind her, staring provocatively at her rear end.

Alana turned around suddenly and flashed him a huge smile. She was surprised to see a camera in his hand.

"Gotcha!" Connor said with a grin.

"Hey, no fair!" Alana exclaimed. "I didn't have any warning."

"I take candids, remember?" Connor asked. "By definition there are no warnings."

"But I probably had my eyes closed or my mouth all weird," Alana said. She walked Nicolette back over toward where Connor was standing. "Let me see," she insisted, trying to peer over his shoulder at the image.

"Oh no you don't," Connor said. "No one sees my photos until I get a good look at them."

"Is that some sort of artists' rule or something?" Alana asked him.

"It's my rule," he said. "Besides, I like you with your eyes closed. You know you always close your eyes when you kiss?"

"I do?" Alana hadn't been aware of it.

"Mmhmm," Connor murmured, and to prove it, he kissed her again, this time pressing himself tighter against her as she leaned on a nearby tree.

Yep, it was true. She closed her eyes, all right.

Thank God for the tree, Alana thought as she felt his body pressing against her own and his hand running through her hair. Being this close to him almost made her feel faint.

The soft haze that enveloped her was broken immediately by Nicolette. The poodle was determined to make her presence known. She wedged herself between them once again and then began rubbing her soft, furry body against their calves. Immediately Alana pulled away.

Connor laughed and held his camera up, taking a close-up of her face.

"Oh, come on, now I'm a mess," Alana said, blushing. But she had to admit she wondered what she looked like just after being kissed.

"Yeah," Connor agreed. "But I kind of like you that way."

"Oh, you do, do you?" Alana asked, bending down and using her free hand to pick up a few fallen leaves. She stood up and poured them over his head. "Now who's the mess?" she asked playfully.

"You're asking for it now," Connor said,

grabbing a handful of leaves of his own.

Alana was waiting for a storm of red, yellow, and orange leaves to fall on her. "Come on, Nicolette," she said, playfully pulling on the dog's leash. "Run."

"I'm going to catch you," Connor teased, taking off after them with the leaves in hand.

You already have, Alana thought. *Totally.*

"You want to come up and help me feed Nicolette?" Alana asked Connor later that afternoon as they arrived back at the Beresford.

Connor shook his head. "Your bosses will be back soon, and I don't think they'd appreciate finding me at the apartment."

Alana looked at him strangely. "Why would they care? You're always up there."

"Yeah, but nothing's broken today. And I'd like to keep it that way," Connor said, hitting his head playfully. "They don't need to know I let myself in just to see you."

"I guess you're right," Alana agreed. "What are you doing tomorrow?"

"I have another head-shot session," Connor said. "A girl from The Actors Institute, just starting out."

"Oh," Alana said, trying not to sound too disappointed.

"Wednesday?" Connor asked.

"I've got all four dogs on Wednesdays," Alana reminded him. "They're a handful."

"You're worth it," he assured her.

"I was planning to take them to the dog run at Riverside Park," Alana explained. "I'd rather let them all run around than try to keep them leashed in the park." She glanced down at her knee. Beneath the jeans she still had a little scar from the time the dogs had pulled her through the Ramble.

"I can meet you there," Connor suggested.

"Cool. Do you know where it is?"

"Sure. Around Eighty-seventh Street," he said. "I've been there."

"But you don't have a dog," Alana noted. "Why would you even . . . ?"

"Ever since I met a certain really cute dog walker, I've been doing my research," Connor told her. He bent down and kissed her on the cheek. "Wednesday. At the Riverside run."

As Connor turned and headed toward the subway, Nicolette started to pull on her leash as if she were trying to follow him. "I

Thirteen

know exactly how you feel," Alana whispered to the dog as she led her back into the building.

"Two tall Mocha Frappuccinos," the barista at the Starbucks at Eighty-sixth and Columbus called out.

Immediately Stella jumped up from the table and grabbed the drinks from the counter. "Mmm . . . nectar of the gods," she murmured. "I need mad caffeine tonight. Big English test tomorrow."

"I know," Alana said. "We're having it too. And I've got to read all of *The Great Gatsby* by tomorrow. Good thing it's short."

"Short but intense," Stella warned. "Get the *Cliffs Notes*."

"Gotcha," Alana said, making a mental note to stop at the Barnes & Noble on Broadway to do just that. She looked over at her best friend and sighed. "I feel like I haven't seen you in a million years."

"Not my fault," Stella said. "I've been trying to see you for the past few days. But it's all Connor and the dogs."

Alana knew that was the truth. "I'll make it up to you," she insisted. "I'm going to see a band at the Red Rooster on Friday night. Why don't you come with?"

"You're not bringing Connor?"

It wasn't like Alana hadn't thought about asking him. But she didn't want to be one of those girls who dumped her female friends the minute she got a boyfriend. *If Connor could actually be called her boyfriend.* Alana wasn't exactly sure. "Nope, you're my guest," she assured her best friend.

"Okay, I'll come. As long as you're not trying to fix me up again," Stella told her. "Last time you tried that, I spent a whole night listening to my 'date' talk about you."

Alana made a face. "That wasn't the plan, I swear," she insisted sincerely. "I really was fixing up you guys."

"Chillax," Stella told her. "I know."

"And I swear I will never try to fix you up again," Alana vowed.

"Pinky swear," Stella insisted, holding out her little finger so she and Alana could relive their childhood promise routine.

Alana giggled, crooking her pinky through Stella's. "But you were right about Connor. He's crazy about me, which I still can hardly believe."

Stella eyed her curiously. "Fishing for compliments?" she joked.

Alana shook her head. "No. It's just weird to think someone I like so much can like me just as much. I'm telling you, Stel, it's been amazing!"

"I know. You've told me every last detail." Stella paused and laughed at the redness rising up in Alana's cheeks. "Okay, so maybe not *every* detail. But enough for me to get the picture. Just promise me you're not going to jump into anything. It's not that long after Sammy."

"Oh, I'm totally over Sammy," Alana said. "It would never have worked out—at least not in that forever-and-ever way."

"Yeah, that was a three-year mistake, all right," Stella replied.

"No, not a mistake," Alana corrected her. "More like a learning period. Going out with Sammy made me realize what I do and don't want in a guy. Every experience I've had has led me to where I am today."

"Ooo, very existential," Stella joked. Then she turned serious. "Look, I'm just saying to be careful. No guy is absolutely perfect."

"I never said Connor was . . ."

"Yeah, you did," Stella insisted. "And I'm telling you that no one can be that hot, that creative, and that charming without something being a little bit wrong. I'm not saying don't go out with him; I'm just saying keep your guard up."

Alana frowned slightly. Poor Stella. She'd been so burned by Frank that she didn't trust anyone. And nothing Alana could tell her was going to change that. The only way Stella was ever going to believe in true love was for her to fall head over heels into it.

"Anyway," Stella said, obviously wanting to change subject. "How about helping the recycling club out with newspaper recycling next Sunday? We're all meeting at the school to do the bundles."

Alana didn't answer right away. Instead she took a huge sip of her Frappuccino and stared out the window. Sunday? She hadn't spoken to Connor about the weekend yet. What if he . . .

"Hey, you don't have to let me know this second," Stella said, letting her off the hook. "Just keep the date in the back of your head, okay?"

"Okay," Alana told her. "I'll let you know before Sunday, I promise. But before that, I've got to get through tomorrow's English test. You wanna fill me in on some of the themes in *Great Gatsby*?"

Stella reached into her book bag and

pulled out her tattered copy of the book. It was littered with multicolored Post-its, with each color representing a different theme of literary technique.

"Impressive," Alana complimented her. "I don't know anyone else who goes to all that trouble."

"You also don't know anyone else who's pulling an A in English," Stella reminded her. She shook her head as Alana pulled out a pristine, unmarked copy of the book. "What would you do without me?" she asked, only half teasing.

"I don't even want to think about it," Alana replied.

Alana was completely fried before she even reached the dog run on Wednesday afternoon. Apparently one night was not long enough to completely digest the complexities of F. Scott Fitzgerald's novel. She didn't have high hopes for her English-exam grade. She wouldn't fail, but she wasn't going to come anywhere near the A she was sure Stella would receive.

And then there were the dogs. All four of them. And none of them seemed to have to go to the bathroom at the same time. What should have been a ten-minute walk from Frisky's house had turned into a half-hour marathon of sniffing, stopping, peeing, and pooping.

What made the length of her journey even more interminable was the fact that she knew Connor had promised to meet her at the dog run. If he'd already shown up and not seen her there, he might have thought she'd stood him up. Hopefully, he would call her cell to check, but so far there were no calls.

When she reached the dog run, Connor still wasn't there. Now a darker thought crossed Alana's mind. What if he was standing her up?

"Hey, Bridget," Alana asked as she shut the gate behind her, "have you seen a guy who is about six feet tall with longish brown hair hanging around?"

Bridget shook her head. "Not that I've noticed. What kind of dog does he have?"

"He doesn't have a dog," Alana began. "He . . ."

Just then someone snuck behind Alana and covered her eyes, startling her. "Guess who?" he teased in an obviously disguised voice.

Alana grinned and peeled his hands away. She turned around and . . . "Oh, Leo, it's you," she said, unable to hide her disappointment.

"Gee, glad to see you too, Alana," Leo said with a grimace.

"No, I mean, I am happy you're here, it's just that I was supposed to be meeting someone and he didn't show up," Alana explained feebly.

"Well, then, he's missing the big event," Bridget interrupted

"Big event?" Alana asked.

"Sure, it's my Goldie's third birthday!" Bridget exclaimed, sounding somewhat surprised that Alana and Leo hadn't had the date on their calendars. "I've got a dog cake from the Barkery for all of Goldie's friends. Didn't I tell you guys about the party?"

Leo choked back a laugh. "My invitation must've gotten lost in the mail."

"You're not invited," Bridget told him flatly. "Only dogs. I have treats for Princess and Morpheus, and Alana's four dogs too." She stopped suddenly and looked over at the gate. "And speaking of treats . . . mmm . . . who's that delicious-looking young man?"

Alana followed her gaze, hoping . . . "Connor!" she exclaimed. "You got here."

Connor sauntered over, with his hands in his pockets, his long hair blowing, and a smile that could be seen halfway across Manhattan. He was so incredibly beautiful. Alana felt herself naturally drawn to him, as though he were a magnet and she was steel. She began walking across the gravel yard toward him. But before she could get there, Nicolette came flying through the yard, running so fast she appeared to be nothing more than a black, furry blur. Immediately the dog began jumping up and down to greet Connor. Alana watched as he stopped where he was and bent down to greet her, letting the poodle lick his face for a moment.

"That poodle sure has good taste," Bridget remarked.

"Yeah, she does," Alana agreed. Then she walked over to Connor and Nicolette. "Hope I'm not breaking up this love fest," she teased him.

Connor looked up and grinned. "What can I say? I'm a sucker for brunettes." He stood up and lazily ran a finger through Alana's golden brown locks before kissing her heartily on the lips. "Mmm . . . ," he said playfully. "Your lips taste a whole lot better than Nicolette's."

"I would hope so," Alana told him. "I haven't been eating liver-flavored kibble all afternoon. And *she's* not wearing strawberry-flavored lip gloss."

Connor made a face. "Liver and strawberries. Now, there's a nasty combination." He kissed Alana again. "I'll stick with the berries," he joked.

"Is this the guy you were looking for?" Bridget asked as she walked over toward Alana and Connor.

All my life, Alana thought. But out loud she said, "Yeah. This is Connor. Connor this is Bridget."

"I'm Goldie's mother," Bridget said, pointing to the golden retriever with the cone-shaped hat on her head. "It's her birthday."

"Bridget's having a party for Goldie," Alana explained to Connor.

"And you're just in time," Bridget told him. "Come on, everyone gather around. I stopped at the Barkery and picked up a special dog-friendly cake."

Alana watched as Connor tried to keep the amusement from being too apparent on his face. But by now she could read his eyes. And while he was managing to keep a straight face, his eyes were laughing. Any minute now, he was going to lose it. It was probably best to get him away from Bridget before he did. "Come on, I want to introduce you to someone," she said, pulling him by the hand over to where Leo was standing.

"Connor, this is my friend Leo," Alana said, introducing him. "We're both dog walkers. And Leo, this is Connor . . . ," she said, pausing for a minute, unsure of how to phrase their relationship. "My . . . um . . ."

"I'm the boyfriend," Connor said in a light, relaxed tone. Not at all nasty or territorial, though, the way Sammy had come to be toward the end. Connor was just stating a fact.

Alana could feel that now-familiar tingling running through her body again. *Boyfriend.* He'd said it. With one word, he'd defined their relationship. Now she had no more questions. Alana laced her fingers through his. He winked at her and gave her hand a squeeze.

Alana looked into Leo's eyes to check his expression. Was he surprised she hadn't mentioned having a boyfriend before?

Apparently not. Leo just grinned at her. "Chemistry?" he asked her.

Alana nodded. "Yeah."

"What?" Connor asked, trying to decipher what was going on between the two of them.

"Oh, nothing," Alana told him. "Just an old joke between two dog walkers." She watched Connor's face for a sign of jealousy, like Sammy had shown when she and Leo had spoken that way. But there wasn't a hint of it. Connor seemed perfectly fine with the idea of Alana having friends of the male persuasion. He was secure in himself—which made him that much sexier to her.

"Oh, no, check that out," Leo said, pointing toward the middle of the yard. Suddenly barking could be heard everywhere as the dogs went running toward Bridget.

Bridget was holding the cake in the box. But the dogs' keen sense of smell permeated right through the cardboard. Alana had no idea what was actually in that cake, but whatever it was, the dogs wanted it.

"Get down! Get down!" Bridget shouted.

"Curly! Nicolette! Frisky! Noodles!" Alana shouted. "Come!"

Other dog owners called to their pets as well. But the dogs were way past listening. It was clear the only thing they wanted was that cake. They were jumping higher and higher, barking at Bridget. Finally, it was Goldie who, with one gigantic body slam, knocked her owner to the ground. In a second the cake was in the gravel. A moment later it was gone. Completely scarfed up by the dogs.

"Oh, God. Bridget, I'm so sorry," Alana said as she helped her to her feet.

"We didn't even get to sing 'Happy Birthday' or anything." Bridget looked as though she might cry.

"It's okay. We can sing it now," Alana assured her.

"But you're supposed to sing it *before* you eat the cake," Bridget insisted. "That's how it's always done."

"Goldie doesn't know that," Alana assured her. "Come on. Let's sing."

Bridget looked at her doubtfully but began to sing slowly. "Happy birthday to you. Happy birthday . . ."

As she joined in with Bridget, Alana turned toward Leo and Connor, hoping they, too, would sing. But the boys were standing by the fence, laughing hysterically. As soon as the song was finished, Alana went over to join them.

"You guys are terrible," she said, playfully chastising the two of them.

"I was singing, *really*," Leo joked. "Just in a pitch only dogs could hear."

"Very funny," Alana replied sarcastically.

Connor chose that moment to lean down and plant a gentle kiss on her cheek.

"What was that for?" Alana asked him.

"Because you're sweet," Connor explained. "And because you're the only person I know who could feel sorry for a woman who has too much time on her hands, has too much money, and thinks that the fact that the dogs ate the cake before she could sing 'Happy Birthday' is a real problem. I mean, did you hear anyone else singing?"

Suddenly it hit Alana that she really had been the only person besides Bridget to sing. Which meant everyone in the dog run and the surrounding grass had heard her. She was pretty sure it had not been a pleasant concert. Alana wasn't exactly known for her singing. "I hope the dogs drowned me out," she told the guys feebly.

Leo shook his head. "Uh-uh. We heard it all." Then, noticing the red flush that was once again climbing up Alana's cheeks, he added, "It wasn't so bad. You've got a much better voice than I do. Hey, my gift to the dogs is the fact that I didn't sing. There's a reason I'm with the band and not *in* the band."

"What band?" Connor asked.

"It's this group called Modern Art. I kind of produce them," Leo explained. He looked at Alana. "Are you bringing him to the gig at the Red Rooster on Friday night?"

Alana shifted her weight from one foot to the other. This was awkward. "Um . . . I kind of promised Stella I would bring her," she explained to Connor. "We haven't seen that much of each other lately and . . ."

"Girls night out," Connor said with a shrug. "I get it. She's your best friend."

Alana stared at him in amazement. Sammy never would've understood that. She wasn't sure too many guys would. She reached up and kissed him. "That's for being you," she explained.

"I just wish I didn't have this stupid family thing on Saturday," Connor grumbled. "That means more time away from you."

Alana frowned slightly. *Oh, yeah, the family thing.* He'd mentioned it during one of their phone conversations. He hadn't given her many details, just that it was some huge commitment and that his mom would kill him if he didn't go. Alana understood about stuff like that. Families sometimes got in the way.

Suddenly a loud chorus of barks rang out. Alana shifted her attention over to the far end of the dog run, where Bridget was standing, holding a bag of special Barkery cookies. Naturally the dogs were all over her. That woman just didn't learn her lesson.

"Come on, you dogs, get in line. Wait your turns," Bridget was shouting. But the dogs weren't in the mood to wait. They wanted those treats now.

"Oh, this is too good to pass up," Connor said, pulling a small digital camera from his jacket pocket. He leaped up on a bench and began snapping pictures of Bridget and the dogs.

"He's a photographer," she explained to Leo. Then, seeing that Noodles was about to get into a battle with a Dalmatian over one of the bones, she hurried over to where the dogs were. "I'd better get them out of here," she shouted to Leo.

Noodles was the first dog Alana managed to grab. She fastened his leash onto his collar and then reached for Frisky. But Frisky was no easy catch. He bopped up and down, like a pogo stick. "Frisky! Come here!" Alana shouted. She bent down to grab him, and . . . *boing* . . . she got bopped right in the nose by the hopping Jack Russell.

"Ow!" she cried out, wiping her nose and finding, with relief, that she wasn't bleeding. Her sudden shout caught Frisky by surprise, and he calmed down for a moment—just long enough to be leashed up.

Okay, two down, two to go, Alana thought as she pulled Frisky over to where Curly was calmly watching the goings-on. At first Alana thought that was typical Curly behavior—the prim cocker spaniel seemed the type to be above the fray. But on closer inspection, that wasn't it at all. Rather, she'd managed to get her mouth into Bridget's knapsack and was now happily chowing down on a roll of peppermint Life Savers—paper, aluminum foil, and all.

Alana sighed. Well, at least Curly wouldn't have dog breath today. Quickly she reached over and tried to attach Curly's pink leather leash to her collar. Not an easy task, considering she was holding on to a massive bulldog and pogo-ing Jack Russell at the same time.

Alana's sudden movement startled the cocker spaniel. The dog leaped up high and hit Alana in the leg. Alana was thrown off balance, and in a minute she found herself lying on the ground, surrounded by a bunch of barking dogs. But instead of being afraid or angry, Alana found the whole thing hilarious. At least until she looked down at her arm. There was a big rip in her jacket, and some blood had begun to run down her arm. It was starting to sting. Suddenly it wasn't so funny anymore.

Connor was by her side so quickly, Alana hadn't even seen him coming. Somehow he'd made his way through the pack of barking dogs and leaped into the fray, helping Alana to her feet. Quickly he pulled her over to the bench where she'd been sitting earlier. He opened Nicolette's bottle of Evian and poured water over her wound, using the edge of his blue denim, button-down shirt to blot the wound until the bleeding stopped.

"Oh, no, you're ruining your nice shirt," Alana murmured weakly.

"No big deal. I kind of like brown spots," he said, lifting his shirttail off the wound and taking a look. "It's not so deep. It's stopped bleeding, and I think I've got it pretty cleaned up. Does it hurt much?"

"It stings a little," Alana admitted.

"We should get you out of here and get some Neosporin or something like that on it," he told her. "We'll stop at a drugstore on Broadway and get some Band-Aids, too. I'll have you patched up good as new."

Alana nodded, somehow trusting that he would take care of her no matter what the situation. "You stay here while I go leash up the dogs," he told her. "Then we'll get going."

Alana looked up at him, amazed at the way he'd taken charge of things when everyone else just seemed to be standing there staring at her. It was as though running through a pack of barking, hungry dogs was the most natural thing in the world for him. None of those dogs would have bitten him—at least not in a normal situation. But

Fourteen

when dogs are all keyed up like that—with their sights set on getting food—there can be no telling how they might behave. Connor could have gotten seriously hurt. Yet he hadn't even taken a second to think about his own safety. He'd been too concerned with hers. "You're my knight in shining armor," she told him sincerely.

Connor looked down at his bloodstained shirt. "Actually, it's just cotton from the Gap," he joked.

"Yeah, well, you're my hero, anyway," Alana told him.

"I'm there for you," Connor assured her. "Always."

"Oh, man, this band rocks!" Stella shouted over the music as she and Alana joined the throngs of kids on the dance floor of the Red Rooster on Friday night.

"I know," Alana agreed. She reached up and tightened the ponytail on the top of her head. "I think they're even better than the last time I heard them."

"It was nice of your friend to let us in for free," Stella said. "Where is he, anyway?"

Alana looked around for Leo and finally spotted him in a corner of the room, behind a soundboard. "Over there," she called out over the music. "In the white T-shirt and jeans."

"The guy with the glasses?" Stella asked.

Alana nodded.

"Ooh, he's cute," Stella exclaimed. "You gonna introduce me?"

Alana took another look at Leo. At the moment, he was pushing his glasses back up on the bridge of his nose. One of his short brown curls was sticking up out of his head like an antenna. *Leo, cute? Nice, sure. Smart, definitely. And funny, totally. But cute?* Alana shrugged. There was no accounting for taste. "Of course I'll introduce you," she assured Stella. "Right after this set."

And true to her word, the minute the band announced they were taking a break, Alana hurried over to the soundboard. Stella followed closely behind, nervously fingering one of her long red curls.

"Hey, there!" Alana greeted Leo.

Leo looked up from the soundboard and smiled. "Hi. I thought I saw you on the dance floor. You looked really good out there."

Alana was surprised to discover that Leo wasn't looking at her when he said that. He was staring right into Stella's huge hazel eyes. A connection had definitely been made—at the speed of light. Alana giggled to herself. She hadn't even been planning this as a fix-up. Although she might take credit for it, seeing as it had worked out so well.

"This is Stella, Leo," Alana said, introducing her best friend. "We're on a girls night out. Remember, I told you that was the plan?" she told Leo.

"Hi, Stella," Leo said, never taking his eyes from hers.

Stella lowered her glance shyly and continued twirling one lock of curly red hair. "Hi, Leo. Thanks so much for getting us on the guest list."

"No problem. Smartest move I ever made," Leo assured her. Stella flashed him a demure smile.

"So . . . um, you're working the soundboard tonight?" Stella asked awkwardly.

Leo nodded. "Yeah, the band's trying to make a demo CD, and I'm recording them from the board. It's pretty cool, actually. Let me show you."

Alana stood there for a minute, watching Leo explain the mechanics of recording to her best friend. He seemed so confident and relaxed as he let his hand accidentally-on-purpose brush against hers as he twisted and turned some of the knobs. The action made Stella jump slightly.

How bizarre was this? Stella, who was usually so boisterous and outgoing, now seemed absolutely tongue-tied. And Leo, who never could seem to get his words to come out the way he wanted them to, was absolutely smooth. Life was really weird.

"So are you going to be behind the soundboard all night?" Stella asked him.

"Nah. Not the whole night. I just have to get the first two songs in the next set," Leo told her. "Then I'm finished."

"Oh, that's good," Stella replied. "I

mean, you must be glad you don't have to work the whole time. Because . . . well . . . it's Friday night and . . ."

Alana had to choke back a grin. It was kind of nice to see the usually self-assured Stella be slightly off balance—in a good way.

Just then the band members started making their way back onto the stage. The drummer hit his cymbals, testing the levels. The bass player tuned his top string.

"They're going to start up again in a few seconds," Leo told her.

"Oh," Stella said, sounding disappointed. "Then maybe we should get out of your . . ."

"No," Leo insisted. "You don't have to. I mean, you can hang out here, and I can show you how it really works, if you want."

"That would be great!" Stella exclaimed. Her eyes lit up and her smile completely beamed . . . until she looked over at Alana, remembering for the first time that she was still there. "I mean, do you want to, Alana? Because we can always go dance some more or . . ."

Alana shook her head. "Nah, my feet hurt anyway. I don't know why I wore stiletto boots to go dancing. I'm just going to go get a soda at the bar. And then . . ." The rest of Alana's words were drowned out by the loud sound of Modern Art's next song. Not that it would have mattered. From the looks of things, Stella and Leo were lost in their own world. Anything she might have said to them would have been just background noise anyway.

Alana pushed her way through the throngs of kids toward the bar in an effort to get herself a Diet Coke. It was strange how alone a person could feel in a sea of people. For a second Alana wished she'd made different plans. Instead of a girls night out, she and Connor could be together right now, dancing and laughing and . . .

No! She had to stop those kinds of thoughts right now. She was not going to be one of those girls. Her life was not all wrapped around one guy—no matter how amazing he was. Going out with Stella tonight was a good thing. She'd already gotten some great one-on-one time with her BFF. And more importantly, Stella had smiled in a way she hadn't for a very long time. It was so great to see Stella happy.

Of course, that didn't solve Alana's present dilemma. Frankly, she wasn't looking forward to a whole Friday night of sitting at the bar downing Diet Cokes at three dollars a glass. (And they weren't even Diet Cokes; they were actually Diet Pepsi, which definitely wasn't the same!) On the other hand, she didn't feel like being a third wheel as Stella and Leo did the whole getting-to-know-you thing. And if she just left, Stella would feel awfully guilty. Alana slumped slightly as she leaned against the bar and tried to get the bartender's attention. From where she stood, she could see the dance floor clearly. Everyone out there seemed to be having a great time. So were most of the kids at the bar. Except her, of course. She was bored out of her skull. This evening was in need of some serious rescuing.

And that's when she saw him. Connor! He was coming right toward her, through the throngs of people. At first Alana thought it was a mirage—like the way people who are in the desert believe they see a pool of water that isn't really there. But Connor *was* there. And she was so glad to see him. Once again her knight had come to her rescue.

"Surprise!" he shouted in her ear as he came up to the bar.

"What are you doing here?" she asked him.

Connor frowned slightly at her lack of enthusiasm. "Oh, man, I guess I shouldn't have come. I didn't mean to burst into your plans or anything. I just thought . . ."

"What? No. I am so glad to see you. You have no *idea* how glad I am." Alana flashed him a bright white smile and wrapped her arms around his neck. That perked Connor's spirits immensely. She could tell by the way he kissed her. "How did you know where I was?"

"You and Leo were talking about it at the dog run," Connor explained. "I figured I would just drop by for a few minutes. I couldn't let a whole weekend go by without seeing you. And since I have this stupid family thing tomorrow night, this was the only chance I would have. I hope Stella doesn't get too pissed off."

"Oh, I don't think she'll mind at all," Alana assured him. "She's kind of met someone."

"So much for girls night out, huh?"

Connor asked.

"I guess so," Alana said, her eyes smiling.

Connor let out a huge sigh.

"What was that for?" Alana asked him.

"I guess I'm just relieved. I wouldn't want to ruin your whole night. I didn't want you to think I was one of those boyfriends who have to know where you are every second of the day. I'm not a stalker or anything. I just . . . well . . . I just kind of missed you, and I wanted to see your face for a few minutes."

Alana giggled, crossed her eyes, and stuck out her tongue. "Here it is," she teased him.

"Oh, that's just lovely," Connor teased. He kissed her on the nose. "Worth the price of admission."

The price of admission. Oh, right. Connor had to pay to come in. It was only fifteen dollars, but still. He was just starting out as a photographer, and every dollar counted. He'd spent the cash just to see her for a few minutes.

"And I brought something for you," Connor said, reaching into the inside pocket of his jacket and pulling out a small brown envelope.

Alana took it from him and gingerly removed the snapshot inside. "It's the couple on the boardwalk in Brooklyn you told me about!" she exclaimed. She paused for a moment, unable to move her eyes from the image of the man in the sport jacket and the woman in the lacy dress. These two elderly people were clearly in love. In fact, if you looked beyond the wrinkled lines in their faces and focused on their shining eyes and dreamlike smiles, they could be any young couple in love—except they seemed wiser and more sure of their passion than anyone in a new relationship could ever be.

And somehow Connor had managed to capture all of that with the click of a camera. It was such a hopeful photo. Touching and expressive. Beauty that no one else would have seen. An image that spoke to her. Just like he'd described that night on the park bench.

"I thought you might want a copy," Connor said. "Of all the photos I've ever taken, it's the one I'm most proud of."

And he wanted to share it with her. Alana almost cried. He was so sincere, standing there, waiting for her to say something. Hoping she understood the sentiment in the photo. "I'll treasure it always," she assured him. "It's the most incredible thing I've ever seen. I get it Connor. I really do."

The sheer, unadulterated joy her words brought him was clear from the expression on his face. She grabbed him and hugged him close. Then, out of the corner of her eye, Alana spotted the bartender heading in her direction. If she ordered her drink now, Connor would feel like he had to pay for her. Quickly she put the photo back in its envelope and slipped it into her pocketbook. Then she looked up and planted a kiss on his lips. "Come on," she said, "let's dance."

Connor frowned and glanced at his feet. "There's something you don't know about me," he told her. "I absolutely can't dance."

"I doubt that's true," Alana assured him.

"Oh, it's true. Now, I know you don't believe me because I have such smooth moves everywhere else . . ." He let his voice trail off and grinned as he saw Alana blushing prettily. "But I'm telling you, I'm a lousy dancer. I even do that horrible biting-my-lower-lip and rocking-my-head-back-and-forth thing." To prove it, he started rocking back and forth, in probably the worst exhibition of dancing Alana had ever seen.

But she didn't care. Not one bit. In fact, she was thrilled to learn that Connor wasn't perfect. And the fact that he was willing to make a complete idiot out of himself on the dance floor just because it made her smile, made him all the more wonderful.

It wasn't until the end of the second set that Alana noticed Stella was MIA. She and Leo had obviously left the soundboard after he'd recorded the first two songs of the set. And now they couldn't be found anywhere.

"Maybe she went home without you," Connor suggested.

"Stella would never do that," Alana insisted. "Even if she got sick or something, she'd still find me or text me to let me know she had to go." She pulled out her cell phone to check for a text. "Nope."

"Then she's got to be here somewhere," Connor told her. "We just have to find her."

"She was with Leo last time I saw her," Alana said. "Maybe he took her some place where the band hangs out. Like a VIP room. He might do that if he was trying to impress her."

Connor looked around at the shabby couches, scratched up floors, and peeling paint. "You think Stella gets impressed easily?" he joked.

"You know what I mean. It would be a good place for them to hang out and talk. Get to know each other." Alana pointed to a stairway near the back of the club. "Maybe they went up there." She hurried over and started up the stairs. Connor followed closely behind. She stopped suddenly as a weird sound became audible. At first it was low and rumbly, and then it became louder and gravelly. Kind of like a dog barking or something.

"What is that?" Connor asked.

"I don't know," Alana said. "And I'm not sure I want to find out."

"Whatever it is, it's coming from behind that door," Connor said, moving his way ahead of Alana on the stairs, to ensure that he'd be the one faced by whatever was behind the door before she was. He eased the door open slowly and peeked inside the dimly lit room. He looked inside for a moment and then shut the door before bursting out laughing.

"What, what is it?" Alana asked. She

listened at the doorway as another gravelly bark became audible.

"Oh, you don't want to see this," Connor insisted.

"Yes I do," Alana told him, pushing her way toward the door.

"Don't say I didn't warn you," Connor whispered to her as whatever was behind the door barked again.

Alana opened the door and stuck her head into the room. And that's when she saw them—Stella and Leo—making out on the couch in the VIP room. Her red hair was barely covering his face from view. The two of them were so lost in their mutual attraction that neither of them seemed to sense an additional presence in the room.

"Arooooooooooooo!"

Alana jumped back, startled by the noise. She got herself out of that room as quickly as her feet would move. "It's Leo," she whispered in disbelief.

Connor was roaring now. "He's a *barker*," he said between choking fits of laughter. "The guy's a barker."

"It's so bizarre," Alana said. "I don't see how Stella can keep from losing it."

"It doesn't seem to be bothering her," Connor pointed out. "She looked pretty happy to me."

"Ar . . . ar . . . aroooooo!"

Alana covered her ears at the onset of another of Leo's howling yelps. "Oh, man, I can't take this. I have to get her out of there."

"Why?" Connor asked. "She's having a blast. Maybe she likes a guy with animal magnetism."

"He sounds more like a dying wolf," Alana groaned. "And it's got to stop. If we don't leave soon, we're both going to miss our curfew." She stopped for a second, wishing she hadn't said that. Connor wasn't in school anymore. He was out on his own. Technically a grown-up, although he was only eighteen. She didn't want to sound like a baby to him. She didn't want him to look at her as some high school kid, the way Sammy did.

But Connor didn't feel that way. He wasn't the type to look down on anyone. Instead, he was concerned about Alana's safety. "It doesn't appear that Stella cares too much about her curfew right now," Connor said. "But the last thing I want you to do is get in trouble. Let me take you home. You can text Stella and tell her you couldn't find her."

"But I *did* find her," Alana insisted.

"Do you want to let her know you saw— and *heard*—that?" Connor wondered.

Well, when he puts it that way . . . "Okay," Alana agreed. "I don't want to embarrass her or Leo. Although I don't know how I'm going to look him in the eye at the dog run on Monday."

Connor chuckled. "Just ask him if he can talk to the dogs in their own language. You know, kind of like Dr. Dolittle or something."

"You are so bad," Alana said, poking him in the ribs as she followed him down the stairs and out of the club. Along the way she pulled out her phone and sent Stella a very straightforward and nonjudgmental text:

```
Lost track of you and Leo.
Had to get home by curfew.
Call me.
```

"Did you ask her if she had a howlin' good time?" Connor asked. "Or if Leo's bark is worse than his bite?"

"Ouch. That was bad. You have to stop," Alana said, playfully scolding him.

Connor grinned at her and then stepped off the curb, waving his arm.

"What are you doing?" Alana asked him.

"Getting us a cab. You don't want to walk all the way to the Upper West Side, do you?"

"But it's forty blocks to my house," Alana told him. "You know what that would cost in a cab?"

"Don't worry; I've got it," Connor insisted.

"Oh no. I can't let you do that. I'll just take the subway."

"And *I* can't let you do that," Connor told her.

"A cab costs way too much. How about we take the subway together?" Alana suggested. She paused and thought about that for moment. "No, that won't work because then you'd have to take the subway back by yourself. Maybe you could take the bus. This time of night, that's safer."

"A cab's quicker," Connor told her.

"No way. I'm not going to let you spend that kind of cash . . . ," Alana began.

Connor sighed and looked at her face. He was searching for . . . something. Alana wasn't quite sure what it was. "Look, Alana, I can afford it. Honest. The thing is . . . I'm not . . ."

Before he could finish his sentence, a brown and white dog ran up to Alana and began sniffing her leg.

"Rufus!" the dog's owner, a tall, thin, middle-aged woman with dark curly hair, scolded firmly. "Leave that girl alone."

"It's okay." Alana bent down and scratched the little guy behind his ears. "He's adorable. What kind of dog is he?"

"I don't know," the woman told her. "The vet thinks part terrier, part spaniel. And maybe a little shepherd, too. He's not sure. Basically, he's just a dog. We got him from the pound."

"Oh, you lucky little pound puppy," Alana cooed, giving Rufus one more good scratch before standing up.

"I'm the lucky one," the woman assured her as she led Rufus away and down the block.

"That's the kind of dog I want one day,"

Alana told Connor. "Just a sweet, friendly mutt. It makes me so crazy the way the people I work for make such a fuss over their purebred dogs. I can't stand the way those people pay breeders a fortune for purebred puppies when sweet dogs like that need a home. And rescued dogs are always so grateful! Rufus probably doesn't go to some fancy dog spa or eat designer dog biscuits made by French chefs. But he looks happy. I wish rich people would get their priorities straight." She stopped for a moment and looked at Connor. "Sorry, I didn't mean to go off like that. Besides, you wanted to tell me something. What's up?"

Connor frowned. "Nothing. We'd better get going if you insist on taking the subway. The trains don't run on a regular schedule this time of night."

"At the end of the world, you're the last thing I see. . . ." Alana's cell phone blasted her out of her sleep on Saturday morning. She ruefully reached over onto her nightstand and fumbled through the lipstick, eyeliner, and nail polish until she finally got her hands on it. She flipped open the lid. "Hello," she mumbled.

"Did I wake you up?"

The sound of Stella's voice definitely got Alana's attention. Stella never sounded perky—ever. And especially not first thing in the morning. But "perky" was definitely the only way to describe Stella's tone this morning. Well, maybe "chirpy" would work too.

"No . . . I was just sort of lying here," Alana told her.

"I'm sorry we got separated last night," Stella apologized. "Leo and I were in this room talking, and I guess I just kind of lost track of the time."

Alana choked back a laugh, remembering. Talking? More like barking. Or howling, even.

"He's so incredible, Alana," Stella continued. "Really smart. And cute. I can't believe you didn't fix me up with him earlier."

"I thought you hated fix-ups," Alana said.

"Usually," Stella admitted. "But Leo is definitely the exception to the rule. He's so cool. He wants to be a journalist. I tried to convince him to work for an online newspaper, so he could save trees. At first he tried to convince me that the energy that people use to run their computers isn't exactly eco-friendly, but I said that it was better than killing trees. Then he suggested there be a law that newspapers be made of recycled paper, and I'll tell you, Alana, I got so turned on."

Everyone has her own form of foreplay, Alana thought. Aloud she asked, "So, did you give him your digits?"

"Oh, yeah. And he called already this morning. He's going to come help out tomorrow afternoon with the recycling," Stella replied. She paused for a minute. "Wow. Just the thought of it gave me goose bumps."

"Imagine how you'll feel when you actually see him bundling up the papers," Alana teased.

But Stella didn't seem to catch the humor. "I know. I can't even bring myself to think about it."

Alana knew how she felt. Sometimes she had to fight to keep thoughts of Connor from her mind, just so she could actually function during the day. Of course, at night, when she was asleep, she had no control over her thoughts. She grinned slightly as the dream Stella had woken her from replayed in her mind.

"Are you coming tomorrow?" Stella asked her. "We could use the help. You

Fifteen

could bring Connor."

"I'll be there," Alana replied. "But I don't think Connor can make it. He's got some family thing tonight, and he hasn't actually said anything about Sunday, so I think he probably has things to do."

"Oh, wow. Bummer. You mean you aren't going to get together with him all weekend?"

"I saw him last night," Alana told Stella. "He surprised me and showed up at the Red Rooster."

"I didn't see him," Stella said.

But we definitely saw you, Alana thought, recalling the scene in the darkened lounge. She didn't say anything though. No point embarrassing Stella. Not that Stella embarrassed too easily.

"He came after you and Leo sort of disappeared," Alana explained.

"Did you call him?" Stella wondered.

"No. Somehow he just knew when to show up," Alana said. Connor had a real talent for that. He'd just "shown up" at a point in her life when she really needed someone to show her what love really was about. The Stanhopes were pretty shallow, selfish people. But someday she would have to thank them for living in the Beresford, so that she could meet their handyman. Although people like them probably would never understand why that would be a gift.

"Hello? Alana? Are you there?"

Alana blinked suddenly. "Oh, yeah, sorry. I just was thinking."

"So you want to meet for brunch and debrief?" Stella asked.

"Sure. How about Popovers?" Alana suggested.

"Perfect," Stella said. "It's real close. I don't want to walk too far. I am absolutely dog tired."

Dog tired. After her night with Leo, Alana could understand why.

"Okay, once you've got the papers bundled, just load them onto the truck," Stella explained to the group of volunteers who had gathered at the high school on Sunday afternoon. "Then we'll get them to the recycling center later."

Alana grabbed a spool of twine and began to wrap it around the stack of newspapers she'd gathered. Leo came up beside her, a huge smile on his face.

"You look happy," Alana told him.

"Do I?" Leo asked. The smile grew larger.

"Mmmhmm. Any special reason?"

Leo chuckled. "She's amazing, you know that? I mean, look at her. The way she takes charge is incredible. She's the kind of person everyone looks up to."

"She always has been," Alana told him. "Since we were kids. I swear, our elementary-school teachers used to ask her for advice."

"I believe it," Leo replied. "I wish I had known her then. There wouldn't be so much to learn about her."

"With Stella, what you see is what you get," Alana told him. "She doesn't keep anything hidden."

"I saw her, and it just fit, you know?"

Leo told her. "Like I found the one piece of the puzzle that was missing. What I can't believe is how fast it happened."

Alana could believe it. She knew exactly how Leo felt. One day you're wandering through life, sort of happy but not really, and the next minute, someone appears who makes you feel whole. Someone with unbelievably sexy eyes, tight abs, hair that you just want to run your fingers through . . .

"Alana? How many times are you going to wrap that rope around the papers?" Leo asked her.

Alana looked down. She'd used up half the ball of twine. Man, she really was a ditz these days. Love could do that to a person. "Oh, sorry, I drifted off."

"Yeah, and I'll bet I know where," Leo replied with a laugh. "You were taking a little trip down to Connortown."

Alana flushed slightly and bit her lower lip with embarrassment. "Guilty," she admitted.

"You really like him, huh?" Leo asked.

"Yeah," Alana admitted.

"Well, he'd better be good to you," Leo told her. "Otherwise, Stella and I are coming after him. You deserve the best."

"He's good to me," Alana assured him. "More importantly, he's good *for* me. He's such an incredible person, he makes me want to be better. I mean, I complain all the time about having to pay for part of college next year, and there he is, working so hard to keep his apartment and get his real career going. But he never complains. He just does it."

"Yeah. That is cool," Leo said. "He lives down in the Village, right?"

Alana nodded. "Somewhere near Pomodoro Pizza."

"Pretty nice neighborhood," Leo said. "Not far from my dorm. Wonder how he can afford it?"

"I don't know. Probably a rent-controlled apartment. Or maybe a sublet," Alana replied.

"I wish I could get a deal like that, because I definitely want to stay here for the summer. But the dorms close and . . ."

"The summer?" Alana sounded surprised. "It's only October, Leo."

"I know," he admitted. Then he glanced over at Stella. "But I kinda already know that I'm in this for the long term."

"Oh," Alana said slowly. "Okay. Well,

I'll ask him to keep his eye out for any cheap apartments."

"Or maybe he wants a roommate, just for the summer," Leo said. "I'm very neat. Does he live in a studio or a one bedroom?"

Somehow Alana couldn't imagine Leo and Connor as roommates—even for a few weeks. Connor was so relaxed and laid-back, whereas Leo . . . well . . . Leo was the kind of guy who planned for the summer in October. And as for the apartment, she had no idea. "Um, I'm not sure how many rooms," Alana told him. "I've never been up there, actually."

A smirk formed on Leo's lips. "Not that he hasn't tried to get you there, I imagine."

Alana thought back to the few times Connor had playfully tried to get her to come see his photos at the apartment. But she hadn't gone. She wasn't ready for . . . well . . . for whatever might happen if she and Connor ever found themselves alone in a place with a bed. And she wasn't sure she'd be able to resist him if she were in that position. Not that Connor would ever force anything on her. He was too gentle and kind, too respectful and honorable. But he was also an unbelievable kisser, and their make-out sessions always left her wanting more. Which was exactly why Alana had stayed far from his place.

"Um . . . Leo, can I see you for a second?" Stella called suddenly from the other side of the recycling table.

Leo smiled at the very sound of her voice. "Sure," he called back to her. Then he turned to Alana. "M'lady calls," he said with a bad British accent.

"Then thou had best run," Alana replied with an equally awful one.

She watched as Leo hurried over to Stella and wrapped his arm around her waist as they spoke. Stella seemed to just melt into him, more comfortable and relaxed than Alana had seen her in a long time. It was amazing how quickly that kind of familiarity could occur between two people. They stood there a minute, reading something in the pile of leftover Sunday *New York Post*s Stella was recycling.

They must have noticed Alana staring at them, because they looked over at her for a moment. Alana waved and smiled. But Stella and Leo didn't smile back. Instead, they focused their attention right back to the newspaper.

A moment later Stella walked over to Alana. "How ya doin'?" she asked her.

Alana looked curiously at her best friend. There was something really weird in her tone. "Fine?" she replied. For some reason it came out more as a question than an answer.

"Good," Stella said. She paused for a minute. "Um . . . Alana, what did you say Connor's last name was again?"

Alana paused for a minute. Funny, in the few weeks since she'd met Connor, she'd never asked him that. Then again, he'd never asked her either. It was a detail they'd both sort of forgotten about. It just hadn't seemed important. "You know, I don't know," she told Stella.

"You don't *know*?" Stella sounded incredulous.

"It's never come up," Alana replied matter-of-factly. "Why?"

"Because I think I found out what it is," Stella said. "He's in the paper."

Something in the way Stella looked and sounded suddenly frightened Alana. She could feel the color draining from her face. "Oh my God! Is he okay? Was he in an accident or something? Was he hurt?"

Stella rested a gentle arm on Alana's shoulder. "No. He's fine." Stella reached into her jacket pocket and pulled out a torn piece of the newspaper. "Check this out," she said quietly.

Alana looked at the piece of newsprint. "Page Six?" she asked Stella.

"Look at the picture."

Alana did as she was told. There was a photo of a bunch of rich, society types at a party in the Metropolitan Museum of Art. There was Connor, in a designer tuxedo, laughing and smiling with an older woman. She scanned the caption: MRS. BARBARA STANHOPE SHARES A JOKE WITH HER SON, CONNOR, 18, AT THE BENEFIT FOR THE COSTUME COLLECTION OF THE METROPOLITAN MUSEUM.

Alana blinked hard and then read the copy again. "He-he-he's a Stanhope?" she murmured feebly.

"Looks that way," Stella replied gently.

"But that's impossible," Alana insisted. "I've been in that apartment a million times. I've never once seen his picture anywhere. And Mrs. Stanhope never mentioned having a son when I spoke to her on the phone. Only a daughter, Catherine."

"I don't know about that," Stella said. "All I know is there he is. And that's from this morning's paper. The party was probably the family event he had to go to last night." She stopped for a minute, watching as Alana took it all in. "'It's not that big a deal, 'Lan. 'Stanhope' is just a name. That's all. He's still the same Connor."

"Yeah, Connor *Stanhope*," Alana said, spitting the words out.

"So he's got rich 'rents. Big deal," Stella insisted.

"Snotty, class-conscious, rich 'rents," Alana corrected her.

Stella shrugged. "It's not like he chose them," Stella said. "But he did choose you. And you chose him."

"But why would he say he was a handyman? Why would he want . . ." Alana's head was spinning. She was feeling dizzy and kind of sick. "I . . . I . . . need to sit down," she murmured.

"Why don't we go over and sit on the steps for a minute?" Stella asked, gently leading her to the front of the school building.

"Um . . . no. You keep working. I think

I need to be alone for a minute." Alana walked over to the steps and sat, her eyes never once leaving the newspaper article in her hand. Thoughts began circling in her brain. No wonder Nicolette was so friendly to Connor. He wasn't a stranger. He was part of her family. In fact, he'd probably been the one to walk her after his sister had gone off to Yale. But now that he was out of high school and living in the Village, Mrs. Stanhope had had to hire someone.

Alana's mind was racing now. She thought back to that time he'd taken the orange from the bowl and just started eating it. She'd wondered why he would take food from someone he worked for. But he *didn't* work for them. Mr. and Mrs. Stanhope were his parents. . . . *His parents.*

No. It couldn't be true. It had to be a mistake. Maybe he'd been a waiter or something at that event, and the reporter had gotten it wrong. Or something else. There had to be an explanation. And boy, would he laugh when he found out what Stella had been thinking. Quickly she reached into her pocket, pulled out her cell phone, and dialed the number.

"Hi. Connor here. I'm so bummed I

missed your call. Leave your name and number, and I'll call you back."

Alana frowned as her call went straight to his voice mail. His voice sounded so warm and genuine. Not at all like the voice of a liar. But then again, faking people out was what liars did best, wasn't it?

"Hi, Connor." Alana struggled to keep her voice from shaking. "Can you . . . um . . . give me a call? I need to talk to you about something."

A light rain was starting to fall when Alana emerged from the subway at Columbus Circle. The grayness of the day fit her mood. It had taken Connor three hours to call her back, but when he had, he assured her that he'd meet her anywhere she wanted. She chose Columbus Circle because it was midway between them. *Nobody's turf.* And it was out in the open. Very public. She'd be a lot less likely to scream or cry there.

A yellow cab pulled up at the end of the block, and Connor hopped out. Alana rolled her eyes. A cab. *Of course he'd taken a cab,* she thought ruefully. He could afford it.

Or maybe not. Alana struggled to hold on to hope. Maybe he'd just heard the urgency in her voice and decided to splurge so he could get to her sooner. It was possible. It *had* to be possible.

"Hey," Connor said, giving her a big smile and reaching over to kiss her.

But Alana wasn't about to be kissed by him. Feeling his lips on hers would make it almost impossible for her to get the information she needed. She couldn't resist his touch, and she knew it.

He looked at her quizzically as she pulled away. "Are you all right?"

Alana bit her lip and took a deep breath. "Connor, what's your last name?" she asked him in a cold, clinical voice.

He seemed surprised for a moment and then peered helplessly into her eyes. "I have a feeling you already know the answer to that one," he said quietly.

The knot of emotion that had been trapped in Alana's throat slipped down into her stomach with such a force that she almost lost her balance. "Why didn't you tell me?" she asked him.

"I tried to, I really did," Connor swore.

Alana looked into his eyes. He was telling her the truth. She knew that. But she didn't care. She was too angry. Too hurt. "What? *You didn't get the chance?* We didn't spend enough time together?" she demanded. "We've been together practically every day for the past few weeks. And it's not like you didn't find time for . . . for . . ." She struggled with the words, trying to block his kisses from her mind.

"That's not it," he said, trying to explain. "It's just that the time was never right. I couldn't figure out how to admit to you that I'm related to the snobs who give their dog bottled water and don't offer any to you. That my parents are people who communicate with you through notes instead of face-to-face. Although that one didn't surprise me. That's pretty much how dear old Mom and Dad communicate with me, too."

He stared at the confused look on her face and tried desperately to make her understand. "Don't you think it's odd that they don't have any pictures of me anywhere in that apartment?" Connor asked, his words spilling out at such a speed that Alana could barely understand him. "They can't stand to look at me. Not even a photograph. I'm the big mistake. The one who will never make anything of himself. Not like Catherine. Perfect Catherine. The college soccer star. Division One. The top of the tops. Her photos are on display everywhere. But me? They just pull me out of the woodwork when there's some big event. You know, show the neighbors we're still one big happy family. Except, we're not. They hate that I'm not interested in college, that I don't want to go to business school and become a money man like my dad. It makes them so mad, they can't even stand to look at my picture, never mind spend any long period of time with me in person. Not that that's my idea of a great time either."

"Connor, that doesn't—," Alana began.

But he was on a roll, unable to stop and listen to her. He had a need to make her realize what it was like for him. Why he couldn't bring himself to tell her about his family. "You should have heard my old man when I told him I wanted to be a photographer. 'You'll starve,' he'd said, 'and I can't watch that happen.' So he and my mom basically x-ed me out of their life; even bought me my apartment so they wouldn't have to live with me."

Alana sighed. Well, that explained how Connor could afford to live in the Village on a handyman's salary. Only he *wasn't* a handyman. "Why would you tell me you worked at the Beresford? How could you lie to me like that?"

"I never told you that. Not once," Connor insisted. "You just assumed that."

"Because you were fixing the curtain rod when I met you," Alana recalled.

"I was the one who broke it. A buddy of mine and I were throwing a football around in the living room, and I missed. A mistake. Not the first I've made in that house, or in my life, as my father was quick to point out. But I promised to fix it since my parents don't really trust hired help." His voice was bitter and angry now.

"Hired help *like me*?" Alana demanded.

"No. Not like you. I didn't mean it like that." He rubbed his forehead in frustration and fear. "I don't even know what I'm saying at this point. Alana, believe me, my parents aren't fit to walk on the same planet as you."

"You could have told me," Alana insisted stubbornly.

"I was afraid to," Connor said.

"Afraid?"

"Yeah. I mean, when was I supposed to

bring it up? When your friends in the pizzeria were making fun of that woman in the park for spending more on her dog food than on charity? Or maybe Friday night, when you were going on and on about rich people who get their dogs from fancy breeders instead of picking up strays at the pound?" Connor stopped for a minute and stared at her. He needed to make her see. "Those people you were talking about were my parents. Or people just like my parents. And you hate them. I didn't want you to hate me, too. I didn't want you to think I was a spoiled brat. I'm not, really. I mean, how can you be spoiled when your parents don't support any of your decisions?"

"Are you kidding?" Alana demanded. "They bought you an apartment so you wouldn't have to worry about making a living. You could just go and do your photography. Do you have any idea how many artists would kill for that? To not have to have a day job?"

Connor gasped, and a look of pain came across his face. The idea that Alana had supported his parents was visibly painful to him. All he could manage was a feeble "Point taken" in response.

Alana instantly felt awful. She knew it was more than money and a place to live that Connor was craving from his parents. But right now she was too angry, too hurt . . .

Connor regained his ability to think in a moment and looked her in the eye. "How can you take their side in anything? You know how easy it is for people like my folks to throw money at a problem. It's nothing to them. Like spending money at a private dog-training school . . . remember? You really looked down your nose at that sort of thing. So how could I have told you?"

Alana took a deep breath. She felt as though she were drowning. There was something to what he was saying. She *had* been pretty cold and judgmental about the people whose dogs she walked. And maybe someday she'd be able to understand how he'd felt when she'd talked about them that way. How personally he had taken it. But she wasn't ready for that kind of introspection; not now. All she knew at this moment was that he'd lied to her about who he was. And that made her wonder what else in their relationship had been a lie.

It was raining harder now. Alana was glad, because Connor couldn't tell if it was

Sixteen

rainwater or tears flowing down her cheeks. But Alana knew, and she was powerless to stop the burning, salty water from racing down her cheeks.

"Boy, you must have gotten a good laugh out of my trying to save you money," she snarled, refusing to soften despite the fact that Connor's relationship with his parents was the stuff nightmares were made of. If it had been any other guy telling her the story, she would have been there for him, trying to make him feel better about his family and his life. But she was too hurt. And her feelings were still too raw for her to feel anything but anger. "A trip on the *ferry*. Boy, you must have found that hilarious."

"I didn't suggest we do that. *You* did," Connor reminded her. "I would have taken you anywhere, done anything, if it would have made you happy."

Alana stopped for a minute, realizing he'd just used the past tense to describe their relationship. It probably hadn't been on purpose, but Alana knew it was the right tense to use. "What'd you do after you got home, invite all your rich friends over for caviar and Chardonnay and tell them how you pawed me on the Staten Island Ferry?" she demanded.

That last one hit him like a slap across the face. "*Pawed* you?" He stood there, staring at her, his face turning white and pained. "Alana," he murmured helplessly. "I would never . . . you know me better than that."

"No, I don't," Alana told him, the words getting caught in her tears. "I don't know you at all. I don't think I ever did."

And with that, she turned and began walking back up Broadway, toward her home. She heard him calling after her, but she never turned around.

Alana made two phone calls that evening. The first was to Mrs. Stanhope, telling her that she could no longer walk Nicolette. She didn't offer much of an explanation other than to say that her schedule was too busy, what with college applications and SATs coming up. What else was she supposed to say—I can't risk running into your son? She wasn't even supposed to know the Stanhope's *had* a son. And if people like that found out that their wayward son had been dating their dog walker . . . well, she could only imagine their reaction. And frankly, she didn't want to cause Connor any more trouble. Despite it all, she owed him at least that.

The other call was to Stella, of course. Her best friend was the one she always turned to. Stella was the one person Alana could count on to always understand.

Until today, that is. In fact, Stella acted as though Alana were the one who was wrong. "Are you nuts?" Stella asked her. "You find a guy who is so perfect for you, and you dump him because of who his parents are?"

"No, not because of who his parents are," Alana insisted. "Because *he didn't tell me* who his parents are."

"Okay, that was majorly lousy of him," Stella allowed. "But do you blame the guy? If those were my parents, I'd want to separate myself from them too. The Stanhopes treated you like crap—leaving you those stupid notes and making you cut steak into little pieces for their precious dog. If you were Connor, would you want someone you were just getting to know—*just falling in love with*—to think you were related to *them*?"

"Come on. I'm not that judgmental."

"Yeah, you are," Stella told her. "And so am I. We're kind of reverse snobs. And we're also lucky. We have parents who are human. They would never just cut us out of their lives because we were following our own dreams instead of the ones they had for us. Hell, the only reason his mother probably dragged him to that party at the Met was because it would be easier than explaining what a 'disappointment' her son the photographer was to her. Come on, Alana, you know it's easy for us to be honest about where we come from. Our 'rents are pretty great."

"But he should've known that I . . . ,"

Alana began feebly. She was running out of things to say. Why was Stella defending Connor? Just a few weeks ago she was warning Alana to be careful before jumping into a relationship. What had changed?

And then it hit her. *Leo.* Stella had totally fallen in love at first sight. So now she had no problem with someone jumping into a relationship headfirst. She had a whole different outlook on love now. But this wasn't the same thing. Leo was honest, upfront. A genuinely good guy. All the things Alana had thought Connor was.

"Look, you have to do what feels right," Stella told her. "And I'm not saying you don't have a reason to be plenty mad at him. But break it off? That was a pretty radical move, 'Lan."

Alana refused to be dissuaded. "This isn't the end of the world," she said, trying to convince herself as much as Stella. "I was spending too much time with Connor anyway. I should be focusing on getting my semester grades in shape. They're the last thing colleges see before acceptances. And now I'll have more time to dedicate to working at Helping House and down at the dog shelter where Leo works."

"Okay, Alana," Stella said quietly. "Whatever you want. It's your decision. And I've always got your back. Leo does too. We're there for you."

Alana was true to her word. From that moment on she was the hardest working girl in New York. The most natural place for her to put her energy and time was Helping House. So whenever she wasn't walking Noodles, Frisky, or Curly, she buried herself in her work with the families who were currently living there.

Amazingly, hanging out with the folks at Helping House really did take her mind off her troubles. Compared to what those people had seen, losing a boyfriend seemed pretty small. Besides, Alana was amazed at how distracting playing board games with the little kids could be. Monopoly could be all-consuming if you let it be. And boy, some of those kids were good at buying and selling real estate. The mini Donald Trumps whipped her butt in the game more than once!

When she wasn't going directly to jail and not collecting two hundred dollars on the Monopoly board, Alana busied herself teaching some of the Helping House moms how to knit. It was something Alana had learned as a kid from her grandmother. Actually, she'd never really gotten past the scarf stage, but that seemed to be enough for the struggling women who were taking refuge at Helping House. They didn't seem to care what they were making as long as their hands were busy and their minds were occupied for a while. Alana knew exactly how that felt.

While the mothers at Helping House were grateful for Alana's attention, they were all quite aware that Helping House was doing as much for Alana as she was doing for the organization. They also knew that the lonely seventeen-year-old was far too dependent on her work there. And after a few weeks, they told her so.

"You know, sooner or later you're going to have to face whatever's goin' on," Becky, one of the mothers, told Alana one afternoon during a knitting session. "You can't hide away in here forever. We all have to go out there and move on some-time, kiddo. You've spent the past three weeks here with us every day. That's not normal. You're a kid, Alana. Go out and enjoy life."

Becky's comment shocked Alana. Three weeks? Had it really been three weeks since she and Connor had . . . *broken up*? God, she hated the sound of those words. But that was what had happened, and she had to call it what it was.

Besides, whatever words she used to explain what had happened, the pain of the breakup hurt like hell. At least while she was working at Helping House, she could focus on something else. But now she was being rejected by the women at Helping House. Well, not rejected, actually. Deep in her heart, Alana knew Becky wasn't being mean or anything. She was just pushing her out of the security of the nest and back into the world.

But the world was a cold, heartless place. Out there, there was no hiding from the fact that she was utterly and completely alone. Alana had never noticed before just how many couples there were in New York City. They were everywhere. Kissing. Holding hands. Exchanging loving glances over tables in restaurants. And every single one of those couples seemed to be thumbing their noses at Alana. It was like they were living, breathing billboards in Times Square—flashing neon lights advertising, WE'RE IN LOVE AND YOU'RE NOT! Alana tried hard not to begrudge anyone happiness. But it wasn't easy. Especially when two of those romantic lovers were her two best friends, Stella and Leo.

Up until recently Stella hadn't exactly been a dog lover. But now that Leo was in her life, she'd suddenly turned into Captain Canine, turning up at the dog run with him and volunteering at Operation Dog Adoption. Basically, Stella had invaded Alana's turf. And much as she tried not to feel that way, Alana resented having her best friend around so much.

Not that Stella was *trying* to be mean or anything. In fact, she and Leo worked really hard not to make Alana feel like a third wheel. They never failed to ask her to join them for dim sum in Chinatown after they'd all worked their shifts with the pound puppies at Operation Dog Adoption. But egg rolls and crystal dumplings were little comfort—especially since Alana sat there and ate what she had ordered, while Leo and Stella shared, intimately eating off of each other's plates. She'd never realized before how such a small act could make such a large statement. And yet it did.

That was the thing about relationships. It was the little loving actions that made it clear you were a couple—like the way Stella would pick dog hairs from Leo's jacket collar or the way he would use his napkin to wipe a little drop of duck sauce from the corner of her mouth. And all the while, Alana sat there, alone. A fur-covered, duck-sauce-mouthed, lonely mess.

In the end, the place Alana seemed most comfortable was in her own room. Burying herself in her schoolwork was a win-win situation. Her grades went up, and she could be alone. And as long as she kept her door shut, she could avoid the worried glances from her parents as they passed by her small room. It was hard seeing their concerned faces in the hallway. She knew they wanted to help her, but this just wasn't the kind of thing a girl talked about with her parents. Even physics homework would be easier than telling her mom and dad how much she missed having Connor's arms around her or seeing his smile as he spotted her walking down the block.

So physics it was. Alana concentrated on

Seventeen

bringing up her grade in her toughest class. She stayed after school for extra lab time, studied for hours for exams, and took on the challenge of bonus problems she never would have considered even looking at the month before.

Anything to keep her mind off Connor.

That wasn't easy. The boy was nothing if not determined. He called her endlessly, leaving a trail of missed calls, text messages, and voice mails that remained unanswered. Alana couldn't talk to him, knowing full well that the very sound of his voice would bring back a flood of memories and feelings—like the vision of him with leaves in his hair in the Ramble. Or the way he'd come to her rescue and taken care of her that day in the dog park. Or the awful way he'd danced on the tight, steamy dance floor of the Red Rooster. She'd never felt as happy or as safe as when she'd been with Connor. But it was a feeling she would have to force herself to forget, because remembering hurt too much.

But making herself put all thoughts of Connor out of her mind never worked. Because invariably, at some point, Alana was forced to face her feelings. Whether it was late at night when she was lying in bed, waiting for sleep to come, or during some particularly boring class when her mind drifted off, sooner or later it all came back to her. And when she was alone in her room, it was hard for her not to reach into her drawer and pull out the photo he'd given her. The old couple. A love that lasted forever. Something she and Connor should have had, but never would.

Alana couldn't stay in her room pretending to be a mini Einstein forever. For one thing, she was too into her hair to actually do the whole mad-scientist thing justice. And besides, she knew deep down that hiding behind a physics book was really no different from hiding behind a Monopoly board at Helping House or a dog leash at Operation Dog Adoption. There comes a time in every girl's life when she has to dust herself off and start over. By mid-November Alana had reached that point. She'd had a life before Connor. And she would have one after. It was up to her whether that was a life of sadness and loneliness or a life full of opportunities and adventure.

So when Stella called and asked her to volunteer to work at Operation Dog Adoption's annual November benefit, Alana finally acquiesced and allowed her two best buds to drag her out for a night of glamour and hard work.

Well, not *hard* work, really. Actually, it was kind of fun sitting behind the welcome desk in the downstairs lobby of the Tribeca Terrace, greeting well-heeled guests. She directed them either up to the ballroom where they could enjoy food, drink, and the music of a full orchestra, or up to the roof where they could enjoy the most spectacular, glorious view of the city.

Of course, those destinations were just for the wealthy guests. Volunteers like Leo, Stella, and Alana were relegated to the lobby. Still, Alana smiled brightly as she greeted the men and women in their tuxedos and designer gowns. She was genuinely glad to see them. After all, those people had given a lot of money to the shelter in order to attend the party. This fundraiser was going to earn Operation Dog Adoption enough money to open a second shelter in Brooklyn. In the past few months, Alana had softened a bit. She'd come to realize that it didn't matter whether people gave their time or their money. Just so long as they cared enough to give. Charities needed both kinds of people to keep them running.

And besides, it was kind of fun to be part of the glamour of the evening. She'd gotten all dressed up in a gorgeous red dress with a skirt that blew up like a parachute when she twirled around on her sexy, black stiletto heels. She'd even pulled her long hair back into a glamorous French twist. Alana knew she wasn't actually going to be at the party, but she'd decided to get into the spirit of the evening—even if it did take some major coaxing on Stella's part to get her to pump up the volume on the glamour. Now she was kind of glad she'd listened to her best friend. Being all glammed up made Alana feel like this was the kind of night where anything might happen. Maybe that was why Alana wasn't completely surprised when she heard his voice . . .

"Alana . . ."

Alana looked up from her copy of the guest list and gasped slightly. Connor had always looked hot in jeans and a T-shirt. But in a tuxedo he was downright breath-taking. Just the sight of him made Alana weak. She was glad she was sitting down, so he wouldn't know the power he still had over her. And thank goodness for the long white tablecloth that was draped over the table, blocking the view of her legs shaking up and down nervously. *Incredible.* After all this time, he still had that effect on her.

"Connor. What are you . . . um . . . ?"

Alana stammered. She began turning the pages of her guest list, frantically searching for his name. She kept her eyes on the paper, running her finger down the list of *S* names. That way she didn't have to look into those deep brown eyes that always seemed to see right through her body and into her soul. "Um . . . you're not on the list," she said finally. "There must be some mistake."

"No. No mistake," Connor said. "I'm not a guest."

She looked at his tuxedo. "But . . ."

"I'm the photographer," he told her. "I've been up at the party all night taking candid shots of the guests."

"The photographer?"

Connor nodded. "Did you forget that's what I do?"

No. She hadn't forgotten. She hadn't forgotten anything about him.

"I had some pictures in my portfolio of this adorable dog walker and her dogs. They loved them. In fact, they blew them up to poster size and used them to decorate the room upstairs. Then they hired me to work the event. Well, not hired me, actually. I'm volunteering. But it's a really good cause and . . . I knew you'd be here."

Alana stared at him for a minute. Not sure what to say. "There are pictures of me up there?" she asked finally. *Okay, not the smartest comment, but it's all I can think of at the moment.*

"Who else? You're cute. In fact, you totally upstage the dogs, if you ask me." His voice was slightly strained, as though he was trying unsuccessfully to sound calm and confident. It was clear he was neither of those things.

Alana could feel her heart pounding as he spoke. God, he could be charming when he wanted to be. The familiar tingle of excitement raced through her veins. She tried to fight the attraction, but she was helpless. He was here. In the flesh. And despite everything, it was taking all of her self-control to keep from jumping up and grabbing him.

"Listen, I'm on a break right now while everyone's eating. Do you think we could talk for a few minutes?" Connor asked in a low voice.

Alana swallowed hard. "I'm kind of working and . . ."

"Go ahead, Alana," Stella urged. "Everyone who's coming is pretty much already here. Leo and I can handle any stragglers without you."

Alana eyed her best friend suspiciously. It suddenly dawned on her that Stella didn't seem at all surprised by Connor's appearance at the benefit. Neither did Leo. Which led Alana to believe the two of them had had something to do with this. They obviously weren't going to help her find an excuse not to talk to Connor. There was no getting out of it.

Not that Alana was sure she wanted to. She stood up and, as if in a dream, followed him toward the elevator. As the door slid closed behind them, Alana took pains to stand as far from him as possible, knowing full well she might melt if she even touched so much as his hand.

The doors opened, and Alana followed Connor out onto the rooftop. It was a cool, clear night, and the whole city lay in front of them. "It's like we're above the stars," Alana murmured, staring at the twinkling bright lights below. "This view is magnificent."

"So are you," Connor said. He took a deep breath. "God, Alana, I've missed you, so much."

She just kept staring at the Empire State Building in the distance.

"How have you been?" Connor asked gently.

Alana turned to face him and forced a smile to her face. "I got into Hunter College, early decision. That was a relief. Once I found out about that, I've been able to relax. So I've been just . . . well . . . great."

"Hunter, that's terrific," Connor said quietly.

"Yeah, it's much cheaper than any other school I applied to, so I can give up the dog walking when I start there," Alana continued, babbling about anything but what he really wanted to talk about.

"I thought you'd already given it up," Connor said. "My mother . . . well, she said you stopped taking care of Nicolette."

Alana breathed heavily. "Yeah. I sort of had to do that. I didn't . . ."

"You didn't want to run into me." As Connor finished her thought, his eyes grew kind of glassy, and for a moment Alana thought he might cry. "You never answered any of my calls or messages," he added sadly.

Alana looked away. She knew that was true. She also knew that she'd never deleted a single one—and that there were nights where she'd replayed those messages over and over again, just to hear the sound of his voice. "It would have been too hard," she whispered.

"It doesn't have to be," Connor told her. "I made a mistake. I know. But I was . . ." He stopped and corrected himself. "I *am* so in love with you."

Alana gasped. He loved her. He said it. There was a time she would have been so happy to hear those words coming from him. But right now, she was too confused. A million feelings were rushing through her at once.

"You should have trusted me," she insisted quietly.

"Trust is hard," Connor admitted. "I come from a world where people basically disown you just for having your own dreams. I was afraid to imagine what you might do if you found out who I was. And then, when the lying went on so long, I wasn't sure how to get out of it without losing you." He paused and stared into her eyes. "Please tell me I haven't lost you. Please tell me we can fix this. Because you're the best thing that's ever happened to me. And without you, nothing else really matters. I'm so, so sorry, Alana. Truly."

Alana stared at him. He may have lied to her in the past, but he wasn't lying about this. She could see it in his face. He was trusting her with his heart. And she loved him too much to break that trust. Despite it all, *she loved him*.

She was shaking now, and the tears were starting. But this time they were tears of relief. The long, painful weeks of missing him were over. "I love you," she murmured in a voice so low Connor could barely hear her.

He grabbed her then and held her close, as if he were afraid to let go. Alana stayed there, safe in his arms, feeling herself give way to the fountain of pent-up emotions that were flowing out of her. When he bent down to kiss her, she pressed her lips against his, as though making up for lost time. They clung to each other for dear life, swaying slightly in the same rhythm, beneath the bright moon above. For a moment there didn't seem to be anyone else in the world. . . .

"Hey, Connor, they need you downstairs."

Leo's voice seemed to come out of nowhere. Alana caught her breath and slowly pulled away from Connor as he released his grip on her body. "I forgot you were working tonight," she whispered breathlessly.

"I almost did too," he said quietly. "Will you still be here when I'm finished?"

"Just try and get rid of me," Alana replied.

"Never." He looked at her and smiled. Then he kissed her playfully on the forehead. "After this shindig you can come down to the Village and help me walk my dog."

Alana looked at him with surprise. "You got a dog?"

Connor nodded. "Leo convinced me to adopt her. She's the cutest mutt. Some sort of beagle mix. Her name's Delancey."

"Delancey?" Alana repeated. Then she laughed. "Uh-oh. Be careful. She's a runner."

"She started out that way. But not anymore," Connor assured her. "It wasn't easy, but we've gotten to the point where she trusts me enough to stay in my life."

Alana grinned. "Smart dog," she said, knowing full well that they weren't really talking about Delancey at all. "Lucky, too. To have you in her life, I mean."

Connor's eyes twinkled in the moonlight. "I'm the lucky one," he said.

"We both are," Alana assured him. "And we always will be."

About the Author

Nancy Krulik is the author of more than one hundred books for young readers, including three *New York Times* bestsellers. Her other Romantic Comedies include *Ripped at the Seams* and *She's Got the Beat*. Nancy lives with her family in New York, New York, not far from the Riverside Park dog run, where she takes her crazed cocker spaniel, Pepper, for a run once in a while. She swears she's never taken him to the Posh Puppy, though she has thought about it.

It seemed like the perfect plan—get my boyfriend to fall for another girl, and I'd be free. No muss, no fuss, no guilt or bad feelings.

I approached it logically, like the scientific person I am. I identified the problem. I came up with a hypothesis. I set up an experiment.

And now the results were sitting across the warm, garlic-scented, holiday-bedecked room from me. Or, rather, getting up and walking out of said room, namely Manfredi's, my hometown's fanciest restaurant.

Cam glanced over toward me as he was helping his new girlfriend, Jaylene, with her coat. He smiled and waved. I returned the smile weakly and wriggled my fingers in return.

"What are you looking at, Lexi?" My date, Andrew Cole, stopped talking about himself just long enough to notice I wasn't hanging on his every word. He looked over at the door just in time to see the happy couple depart. "Oh." He shrugged, then shoveled in a mouthful of lasagna before returning to his favorite topic. "So anyway, like I was saying, the admissions guys from Northwestern told me that if I applied, he was positive I'd get in, and . . ."

I picked up my fork and poked at my pasta. But my stomach recoiled at the thought of actually eating it. I'd lost my appetite the second I'd walked into the restaurant and spotted Cam and Jaylene together.

Andrew had, in his efficient, over-achiever way, procured us a great table by the front window. It was tinted with fake frost and draped with garlands of holly and ivy, but that wasn't enough to block my view of Cam and Jaylene as they emerged onto the sidewalk outside. I watched them out of the corner of my eye, not wanting to see any more but unable to resist. Call it scientific curiosity.

It was early December and the tempera-ture out there was normal for late evening in our part of Wisconsin. In other words, frigid. A few snowflakes drifted lazily down,